EYES OF THE HIDDEN WORLD

RYAN KIRK

WATERSTONE
MEDIA

For Chad

PROLOGUE

High on a nameless mountain, death stalked Tomas' trail, hunting the warrior like a relentless bloodhound.

Tomas climbed, hoping to outmaneuver his old nemesis one more time.

His fingers bled as he pinched a tiny projection of stone with his right hand.

He kept his body pressed tight against the cold rock as the wind whipped across the sheer face. It tried to separate man and mountain, seeking any crack it could wedge wider.

Tomas let go of the hold he'd been grasping with his left hand. Thick clouds overhead obscured Tolkin's face, nearly blinding him to whatever awaited above. He crawled his hand up the rock, fingertips searching for the next hold.

He heard the wind building to his left. Trees that had been swaying now groaned and creaked as the gust bent them over. It hit him a moment later, and he felt his hips peeling away from the stone. Blood made his tenuous grip slick.

They waited for him below. A nightmare menagerie of

predators. If the fall didn't kill him, they would. It didn't want him on this mountain anymore.

His left hand scrambled, seeking anything that would keep him glued to the wall.

There, above him, his middle finger found a little pocket in the stone, barely large enough for three fingers. He jammed his fingers in, tightened his grip, and held his position.

A moment later the gust passed, moaning at its failure.

Fingers secure, he lifted his right foot up to a thin ledge he'd used for his hands a minute ago.

It wasn't much, but after what he'd just climbed, the ledge felt like a plateau.

He looked up. The climb above was easier, but not easy. The holds grew larger, and a crack running down the rock whispered a promise of an easier ascent. But a single mistake would still put him at the bottom of the cliff. His arms and legs were heavy with exhaustion. He refused to look down.

"Want help?" Elzeth asked.

Some dangers frightened him far more than falling to his death. "No."

Elzeth rumbled but didn't argue. They both knew Tomas couldn't spare the focus.

He mapped out a route in his mind, imagining the moves he would have to make. Then he climbed.

As the holds became more numerous and easier to grip, a new temptation threatened him. The desire to be off this cliff made him want to hurry, to scramble to the top and collapse, exhausted, on the trail above.

In haste, mistakes were likely, and it only took one to fall to his death below. He forced himself to focus on every move.

Sweat mixed with blood. Sharp stone ripped and caught at his clothing. His forearms burned.

He climbed on.

"One's coming," Elzeth said, calm enough one might believe he hadn't just doomed their whole climb.

"Hells," Tomas cursed.

He was only a bit over halfway up.

"And another," Elzeth added.

Tomas climbed faster, but for every foot he ascended, his heart sank further. He'd seen them climb and knew he couldn't match their speed. He risked a look down.

Two creatures followed him, climbing up the face he'd struggled against with the ease of a pair of mountain goats. They were shaped like enormous spiders, hooked appendages grasping every hold and crack without problem. He imagined those same hooks tearing through his skin.

Far beneath the spiders, the undergrowth of the woods rippled with movement. Countless creatures searched for him. However they communicated, word hadn't yet reached the others about his position far above them.

Hope remained.

A thin thread, perhaps, with a pair of shears hovering dangerously near. But hope, nevertheless.

Tomas pulled himself higher, finding an even wider ledge he could balance on without needing to grip the rock with his hands. He held on anyway and twisted to meet his assailants.

They reached him a few seconds later. He kicked out, catching the one in the lead just before it could hook into his leg.

It made no cry as his foot connected with its body.

The force of the kick dislodged its hooks in the stone, and it fell.

Tomas' victorious grin faded when the creature latched back on to the rock a few feet below.

He kicked at the second one, but it had learned from the mistakes of its predecessor. It danced to the side, then jumped on his back.

Sharp hooks tore through his clothing, finding purchase in the muscles of his upper back. Hot needles of pain twisted and sank deeper. Tomas bit back his own cry of agony and suffered in silence. He wouldn't be the one to alert the others below.

He twisted, trusting his life to one hand and foot so that he could smash the creature on his back against the rock. He felt it crunch between his back and the stone, but the hooks didn't release their grip. If anything, the creature held on tighter.

He slammed his back against the wall again, but the angles were wrong. Maybe he hurt the spider, but he wasn't hitting it hard enough to do real damage.

The second creature reached him again. Tomas kicked with his free leg, but couldn't hit it. The spider on his back dug deeper. The one below him jumped onto his leg and wrapped around it, hooks finding purchase in the muscles of his calf.

The thread of hope snapped, cut in half with one decisive cut.

"Elzeth?"

"Yes?" His voice was sweet and innocent, as if he didn't already anticipate Tomas' request.

"I've changed my mind."

"About time."

Tomas feared the moment of transition, the single heart-beat where he couldn't be sure his body would be his own.

In the space of a single breath, the course of a man's entire life could change.

Strength flooded his tired limbs. His vision and hearing sharpened.

And deep below, in the heart of the mountain, something even darker stirred, called to attention by Elzeth.

But Tomas remained, wholly himself. When he had the time, he promised to let out a sigh of relief. For now, it was time to fight.

The spider on his back died first. Tomas slammed it once more against the stone, and this time the hooks lost their grip. The spider fell off him and tumbled down the cliff.

The second one joined the first when he kicked at a jagged stone. It crunched between his shin and the rock, and then it, too, plummeted into the woods below.

There was no point in trying to hide.

It knew where he was, and now the only question was whether it would pursue him this high up the mountain. Tomas scrambled up the remaining face, his grip strong and his balance sure. One small rock broke off in his hand as he grabbed it, but he had enough forward momentum to reach another hold. A minute later he was at the top of the cliff. His destination wasn't far now.

He spared a moment to look down at the challenge he'd just defeated.

And immediately regretted it.

The creatures that had been searching the woods for him now knew where he was, and they were coming for him. A dark mass of countless skittering shadows rose up the sheer side of the cliff.

Others would seek different routes.

He almost let Elzeth rest, then thought better of it. There would be no hiding. Not from this.

He hiked, ever higher.

The monstrous being at the heart of the mountain waited for him. It knew what he wanted, and it would do everything it could to stop him. Unfortunately, it had a lot more friends on this mountain than he did.

As he ran, Tomas only had one thought running through his head.

If he survived this, the next person he passed who asked for help was getting a very different answer.

He was going to tell them "no."

1

Five days earlier

Tomas stared at the house as he scratched at the back of his neck. He stood on a small rise, and his gaze carried for miles. Off in the distance, dark mountains stretched toward the sky, snow-topped peaks melting into the clouds above.

Far below the summits, spring was in the air. A cool west wind blew down from the mountains, but when the sun broke through the clouds, Tomas was tempted to peel off a layer of clothing.

"Seems like a pretty nice place," Elzeth said. "You think this might be a place you want to settle down?"

Tomas looked at the house. "Seems a bit crowded."

Elzeth chuckled. "So we keep going?"

"We do. But maybe we stop here first."

Directly to the south of the house, Tomas counted five people turning the soil and planting seed. He couldn't decide if he should call the plot of land they worked an enormous garden or a small field, but it was one of the two.

Though he couldn't see much of what was behind the house, he occasionally caught the familiar scent of manure on the breeze and assumed animals were involved.

He let himself be silhouetted for a minute. Eventually, one of the figures below spotted him and waved in greeting. Tomas returned the wave and resumed his journey.

Elzeth barely flickered to life. "Expecting any trouble?"

It was always a valid question in these parts. With no law to fear, it was as easy to kill a stranger as it was to break bread with them. And these far frontiers attracted those who hadn't fit well in society in the first place.

But those he crossed paths with tended to be hospitable. There was more than enough space for everyone, and why kill for food and supplies that were offered freely?

Tomas watched as four of the five figures went into the house. The one who remained was the one who had waved. The father, most likely. He went to the side of the house. When he returned, he carried something long and thin.

A rifle, cradled in his arms. No typical settler, then, to be able to afford such protection.

Even from a distance, Tomas could see the weapon was held loosely and pointed down. The father who held it didn't expect to use it, but wanted it at hand.

"I don't think so," Tomas said.

Elzeth returned to the deep slumber that was his normal state of being.

It took Tomas nearly twenty minutes to reach the home. He stopped about thirty feet away from the man and gave a short bow. "Greetings. My name is Tomas."

The farmer matched the bow. "Tatum. If you mean us no harm, be welcome."

"Thank you kindly." Tomas came forward. "Wasn't expecting to find a house this far west."

"We're the last one as far as I'm aware, at least in this area." Tatum's eyes drifted to the sword at Tomas' hip. "You a soldier?"

"Was, once."

"That why you're out here?"

"More or less."

"Wrong side?"

"The government tells me I was, at least."

That brought a grin to Tatum's face. "Well, come on in. I'll introduce you to the family."

Inside, Tomas met Godiva, Tatum's wife, as well as his sons Harlow and Heath and his daughter Wassa. He took an immediate liking to them. Godiva kept glancing at his sword, clearly nervous but too polite to mention it. To ease her mind, he took it off and placed it against a wall by the door. She gave him a small nod of thanks.

He quickly became the children's sole concern. He grinned at their endless questions and offers for assistance. Far from being gracious hosts, he suspected they saw him as a way of getting out of their daily chores. But they brought a smile to his face regardless.

He took the water that Harlow, Tatum's oldest, offered. The other two pulled out a chair for him to sit on, which he gratefully accepted. Tatum sat across from him while Godiva called for the children to help her prepare a lunch. "Do you have any particular destination in mind?"

"Someplace without people."

Tatum laughed. "You've passed through dozens of miles of empty land just to get here. If that's really what you're looking for, you must have been walking with your eyes closed." But he didn't press the matter. People didn't come out this far without a reason, but more often than not, it was one they didn't care to share.

Before long, Tomas found himself at a long table, smiling at the children's stories of life on the frontier. From what he could gather, the family had been here for nearly two years. The conversation quickly became a contest between the children to see who could tell their visitor the most impressive story. Harlow spoke of an enormous bear he'd seen, that he claimed he hadn't been frightened of. Wassa talked about how she helped her mother all day and made the best biscuits.

"My daddy killed a woman," Heath said, a proud smile on his face.

The boisterous table fell silent.

Tomas guessed Heath wasn't more than five, and the child looked around the table, aware he'd done something wrong but not sure what.

Tatum's gaze was turned down, and Godiva cleared her throat. "Tatum was a doctor, back east. A good one, too. One day he lost a patient he was operating on."

Tatum reached out and laid a hand on top of Godiva's. He looked up. "Her brother blamed me. Took it to court, but I was found innocent. So he took justice into his own hands. Turns out, he had friends in the Family. We fled, and he pursued." He let go of Godiva and spread his hands wide. "So here we are."

"Long ways out," Tomas remarked.

"First place we felt safe," Tatum said.

There was a moment of silence. Heath, apparently eager to continue the conversation, pointed at Tomas' sword by the wall. "How 'bout you? You ever kill someone?"

"Heath!" Godiva scolded.

"It's all right," Tomas said. It was an innocent enough question, and Heath was too young to know it was rude. "No," he lied. "I have not. I try to avoid fighting."

"And that's a lesson you all should learn," Godiva said.

They finished their meal, and Tomas stood. "I'm grateful for your hospitality, but I'll be taking my leave now. Don't want to trouble you any more than I already have."

The children groaned, but Tomas caught the look Godiva and Tatum shared. Godiva allowed the children to say their prolonged farewells, then herded them to their chores around the house. They offered him plenty of food for the road, which he accepted. His pack had been getting light the last few days. In return he gave them some hides he'd collected. Tatum accompanied Tomas outside. "You planning on going up into the mountains? Maybe do some prospecting?"

"Might head up the mountain. The idea was just to keep heading west. No interest in prospecting, though. Why?"

"Don't suppose you're the type of man to heed a warning, are you?"

"Depends."

"Don't go up into those mountains. Once you reach them, head south instead. I hear the range isn't so difficult to cross once you've gone a week or two that way."

Tomas looked out at the mountains again. "What's up there?"

"Don't know, but we get a steady trickle of prospectors coming through this way. Maybe a dozen or so in the few months. People who go up there never come back."

"Maybe they're all up there digging gold."

"I don't think so." Tatum hesitated. "You can call me crazy, but there's something else in those mountains. Something unnatural. There's more sagani up there than I've ever seen in one area."

That was an interesting claim.

Tatum must have noticed his look. "Or you can ignore

my warnings. Everyone else does. We just had a lone prospector and daughter come through here the day before last, and they kept right on riding, no matter how I tried to tell them it was no place for a young girl. Got the feeling the man felt he didn't have much choice, though."

"I appreciate the hospitality, and the warning," Tomas said. "I'll admit to being curious about the sagani, though."

Tatum turned and joined him in staring out at the mountains. "If sagani are your interest, I'd advise you to look elsewhere. They aren't right up there."

"What do you mean?"

Tatum didn't answer for a moment. Then he sighed. "I suppose it doesn't matter if you think I'm mad or not." He took a deep breath. "Up there, the sagani are evil."

2

The sun crawled across the sky like a lazy child, warming the world below. Despite the heat of the day, when Tomas now looked to the mountains, he fought the shivers that ran down his spine. The peaks that had once looked majestic now loomed overhead, jagged and mean.

Tomas was not a superstitious man. The world contained more mysteries than knowledge, but that was only because explanations had not yet been found.

Elzeth shared his agitation. His stomach roiled like the great sea on a stormy day.

"Think he's mad?" Tomas asked.

"No," Elzeth said.

"Believer?" The First Church of Holy Water had no love for sagani. They called the mysterious creatures evil.

"He didn't have any of the symbols of the church in his home," Elzeth pointed out.

It wasn't conclusive evidence, but enough for Tomas. Tatum hadn't struck him as a believer. Or mad. Because

Tatum expected Tomas to doubt the warning, Tomas was inclined to believe it.

"Going to take a look?" Elzeth asked.

Tomas grunted. "We'll see when we get there."

A half day of walking brought Tomas to the foothills of the mountain range. The land gradually sloped upward, leading to a line of shorter mountains that guarded the taller peaks behind.

Tomas looked south and saw the route Tatum would have him take. There were no human paths here, but Tomas saw how he might parallel the foothills for many miles. The summits far in the distance looked less tall than those here.

A reasonable choice.

"Tomas," Elzeth warned.

His vision sharpened, and out of the corner of his eye, he saw grass part as something moved through it. He turned his head so that he could watch the new arrival.

It kept low to the ground, revealing only brief flashes of color. When it stopped, there was no sign of its presence.

Tomas waited.

Minutes passed. Tomas' left hand inched toward the hilt of his sword. With his thumb, he loosened the sheath's grip on the weapon. Few creatures in the world were faster than an attacking sagani, and a single moment might mean the difference between life and death.

Elzeth coiled like a spring, ready to blaze to life if needed. Tomas would need the help. Even smaller sagani, as this one promised to be, were deadly.

A small head, modeled after any number of snakes, rose from the grass, just high enough to see Tomas clearly.

The sagani stared at him, and Tomas matched the stare.

No one could say for sure exactly how intelligent the sagani were. From Tomas' own experience with Elzeth, he believed the question was meaningless. Humans tried to measure the sagani's intelligence using a ruler that had humans as the apex. But the sagani were measured on a different ruler entirely. They didn't think as humans did, so any comparison was bound to be futile.

Not that any of the scholars gave his opinion even a second of consideration.

This creature made Tomas doubt, though. He swore he felt a cold intelligence behind its gaze, as human a stare as he'd ever seen.

Even the warmth of the sun felt cold.

Then it was gone. The snake-shaped sagani dipped its head out of sight and it slithered quickly away. West, in the direction of the mountains. Tomas lost it within a few seconds.

"That wasn't like any sagani I've ever met," Elzeth said.

"Agreed." He looked to the south. An easy path, still covered in the light of the falling sun. Then he looked west, his gaze traveling to high places that might have never felt the tread of a human foot.

"I want to go up there," Elzeth said.

"Really?" Of the two of them, Elzeth was most often the sensible one.

"Couldn't tell you why, but yes."

Tomas did, too, but he suspected Elzeth already knew.

He looked again to the south, the grasses turning shades of gold in the early evening. Up ahead, the shadows grew deeper as the sun approached the tips of the peaks.

Tomas sent a silent apology to Tatum, then started the hike up the foothills.

It didn't take long to find the evidence of the passage of other humans. The land funneled humans and animals alike onto predictable paths. Tomas had seen it hundreds of times. On many hills, a traveler could hike straight to the top, but they never did. They zigged and zagged up the slope to keep the incline manageable. Humans cared less about distance and more about the ease of their next step.

The trail he found barely deserved the name. When he first crossed paths with it, he bent down to observe it more closely. Maybe two dozen pairs of feet had beaten the trail over the course of the past year. Not many, but still more than he expected. Horses had been on it recently. He saw a pair of tracks running west, and another pair running east. The set running east looked like they had been galloping.

He followed the trail. Once, he thought he spotted another sagani observing him, but Elzeth was resting, and Tomas wasn't sure.

Before long he heard the familiar sounds of running water. Another couple of minutes of hiking brought him to a small creek. The trail he followed paralleled the creek for a few hundred feet, and then Tomas froze in place.

He sniffed the air, and Elzeth came to life.

The scent was all too familiar. With Elzeth, the power of it stung his nostrils.

Blood.

Tomas drew his sword, more on instinct than reason. It wasn't fresh blood, but who knew what scavengers he might come upon?

He followed the scent, already fearing what he might discover.

His nose led him farther up the trail, to a place where the creek briefly widened into a small pool. Beside the pool, a camp had been made.

Tomas ignored the details of the camp. A body lay near the remains of a fire, mutilated almost beyond recognition.

Tomas approached, studying the scene with an experienced eye. He'd seen too many of the dead in his years, too many ways to die. Whatever had killed the man before him had been particularly vicious.

He squatted down next to the body, ignoring the stench.

"The prospector Tatum told us about?" Elzeth asked.

"Most likely."

"Didn't Tatum say he had a young daughter with him?"

"He did."

"So where is she?"

Tomas looked around the camp. Even a cursory glance was enough to tell him it was empty other than the body. Tomas stood upwind of the miner's corpse and sniffed the air, but didn't catch the scent of any other bodies.

Not a foolproof method, by any means, but curious all the same. He looked back at the body of the prospector.

Tomas didn't think the girl was anywhere near.

3

"Search for her?" Elzeth asked.

Tomas considered for a moment. If nothing else, it gave him an excuse to indulge in his curiosity. "I'd like to."

Elzeth settled into a comfortable slumber. Tomas turned to the camp. If he knew what happened here, it might help him find her.

He returned to the body of the miner, examining both the man and the wounds he'd suffered.

The miner was short and lean. His muscular arms and back told the story of a man who'd spent much of his life swinging pickaxes. He had light hair and an impressive beard, now coated in blood. The absolute lack of fat on his body made Tomas suspect the man wasn't wealthy.

Of course, that almost went without saying. A wealthy man didn't drag his daughter into unknown lands at the barest sliver of hope that he might find a life-changing vein.

The wounds on the body confused Tomas. The prospector had a number of sharp cuts that looked like a sword had inflicted them. But there were more jagged cuts as well, putting Tomas in mind of a claw or talon.

Scavengers had been hard at work on the body, too. There were a lot of parts missing.

From the grotesque expression frozen onto what remained of the man's face, he hadn't died easy.

Tomas looked off in the distance, but the mountains held no answers for him. A group of bandits with dogs, perhaps?

He shook his head. If that had been the case, he would expect to see bite marks from the dogs.

He couldn't say exactly how the man died. Killed was killed, though. He let the problem rest and moved on to the rest of the camp.

Two bedrolls had been placed on the other side of the fire from where the body lay. They were undisturbed, and the first threads of a story began to weave themselves together. One large pack and one small pack lay haphazardly by the bedrolls. They'd been looted.

Tomas went to the packs and looked through them. Clothes remained inside, as did common supplies. A handful of coins had been stuffed near the bottom of the small pack. Near the big pack, Tomas found mining tools, including two sticks of explosive. He took those. They were almost as valuable, and as useful, as bullets.

The only commodity missing was food.

What kind of bandit killed for food and left the explosives and money? Tomas scratched his head.

Nearby, Tomas found bark rubbed off a pine tree where it looked like horses had been tied. The horse tracks leading west ended here and doubled back down. The horses, at least, had escaped the slaughter.

He finished his investigation by making a circle around

the camp, looking for tracks. He found more than he expected. No small number of animals had visited the area recently, and they'd come from several directions. At first, the only human tracks he could find were around the camp and on the trail that led higher up the foothills. If bandits had killed the miner, they'd followed the trail down.

When he approached the pool of water, he found smaller human prints. Barefoot. The right size for a younger girl. They went to the water, then back to the camp.

Tomas frowned and looked across the pool. In the fading light of the day, it wasn't easy to see. He stirred Elzeth to life.

There was a disturbance on the other side of the pool. And small prints, booted.

"She crossed the stream," he announced.

He looked up and down the water channel. It narrowed again higher up, so he ran up and found a place to jump over. He didn't even have to return to the pool. He found her tracks heading west, climbing the foothills.

"Hold on," Elzeth said.

Tomas came to a stop.

"You know what happened?"

"Not exactly," Tomas admitted. "They'd made camp, but they were attacked before falling asleep. So probably late afternoon, early evening. I think the girl was bathing in the pool when the attack happened."

"And they missed her?"

Tomas blinked as he considered the implication. The pool had only been about fifteen feet from the camp. And the bandits had looted both packs. They'd been there for a few minutes, at least, and they would have known a second person was near. "Maybe she's good at hiding?"

"Put yourself in her place," Elzeth said. "If you're a young girl, and your father gets killed in front of you, what are you going to do?"

Tomas looked down the hill at the plains below. "I'd run back to Tatum's. It's the last safe place I saw."

"So why is she running up the hill and away from safety?"

Tomas thought for a few moments more. "Revenge?"

"Possible," Elzeth admitted. "Or she's more scared of Tatum than she is of the mountains."

The idea didn't sit well with Tomas. He considered himself a good judge of character, and Tatum had seemed like a good man.

He couldn't rule out Elzeth's suspicion, as unlikely as it seemed. The mysteries on this mountain were piling up. "I suppose the only way to know is to ask her."

"That attack happened yesterday," Elzeth pointed out. "What are the odds she survived a day without her father, in these mountains?"

It was a question that didn't need answering. Whether the girl was alive or dead, Tomas would search for her. He had to know, and if the girl was alive, he could escort her back to Tatum's place. She'd have a future there, hard as it might be.

He followed the girl's trail. She'd kept close to the stream, leaving muddy footprints whenever she neared too close to its banks.

He supposed sticking to the stream had been wise. Water was life, and lack of it would be the first thing that killed her, assuming nothing else did.

But the path on the other side of the stream was clear to see. The girl might be close to water, but she'd also be easily visible to anyone walking up or down the trail. Like the bandits who killed her father.

A half mile up the stream, he found a disturbance. The girl had broken away from the stream, and from the looks of it, had tried to find a place to sleep.

Her bedroll was back at camp. He imagined her, cold and alone, shivering under the two moons. He wasn't a terribly sympathetic man, but no child should have to endure that.

The good news was, she'd endured the night. Her tracks continued west. If the timeline in his mind was accurate, that had been this morning. Depending on how strong she was, she couldn't be too far ahead of him. If he pushed through the night, he should find her.

The sun set, and for a time, the world was dark. Tomas paused his pursuit. Even with Elzeth, it would be too easy to lose her trail. Tolkin would rise in less than an hour, and then he would have more light to follow her by.

He sat down in the same place where she'd lain the night before and pulled some food from his own pack. Godiva had supplied him well, and her food was delicious. Nothing made a meal taste better than miles of hiking.

Tomas had just finished when he heard something moving in the darkness, across the stream.

A sliver of Tolkin rose in the east, its pale red glow casting dim illumination over the scene.

From the sounds, Tomas had expected an animal.

Instead, he saw a human.

It was a man with unkempt hair and a beard that came almost to his chest. He was filthy, and Tomas caught a scent of him on the breeze that almost made him gag.

Tomas didn't move. In the weak light he didn't think any human eye could spot him in the grass.

The man's head snapped around with unnatural speed.

When it stopped, the man was staring at him. His eyes were wide and possessed no reason.

The man gnashed his teeth, snarled, and charged at Tomas' position. It was only then Tomas caught the dull glint of a bloody knife in the man's hand.

4

The man leaped across the stream and swung his knife with all the grace of a drunken banker. Tomas stepped to the side and the man charged past him as if his actual target was ten paces behind Tomas.

Tomas turned to keep an eye on the man. "Where's the girl?"

The man snarled, the sound emanating deep in his throat. His eyes were unfocused, staring at something behind Tomas. He attacked again, his bloody weapon dark in Tolkin's dim light. Tomas kicked out, catching the man in the chest.

It was like kicking a brick wall, only more painful. And in this case, the brick wall was trying to kill him.

In any reasonable world, the man would have fallen flat on his back. But in this one, the man remained standing, and Tomas stumbled back. The knife slashed again, and this time, Tomas couldn't so easily dodge.

Elzeth flared to life. The knife slowed, and Tomas spun down and out of the way. He hit the ground hard but rolled back to his feet. Better a bruise than a deep cut. Especially one from that knife. It came with an almost guaranteed chance of infection.

His enemy wasn't deterred in the least. The man came for Tomas again, refusing to give Tomas any space to breathe. Tomas retreated as fast as his feet could carry him.

The man followed Tomas without problem.

Which should have been impossible.

Elzeth burned brightly.

Too late, Tomas realized who he fought, as impossible as it should have been.

Tomas wanted to ask how, but no questions would reach the man. Whatever had been human in that body was gone.

Tomas set his stance and lowered his weight. He'd been lucky to avoid the first exchange the way he had. This was not a fight to take lightly. The man would be faster and stronger than Tomas. Nothing was more dangerous than a host, consumed by madness, near the end of their life.

Tomas needed time to draw his own sword, but the man didn't seem interested in providing him any. His greatest advantage was the man's lack of technique and reason. Whatever he had been before, it wasn't a soldier. The man swung at him again, the knife almost invisible. Even with Elzeth, Tomas barely reacted in time. He caught the man's wrist. He couldn't hold it, but he could throw the man off-balance.

So he did. The man crashed to the ground, hard. Tomas was almost tempted to pursue the advantage, but thought better of it. He backed up and drew his sword.

The man rose with unnatural speed. He advanced, the knife carving patterns of madness in the air.

Sword in hand, Tomas ended the fight quickly. Two cuts cost the man his arms. He barely seemed to notice. He lunged at Tomas with his mouth, teeth seeking Tomas' neck.

One final cut took the man's head.

Tomas waited a few extra seconds, ensuring no further surprises were in store. It was hard to tell with hosts. Then he cleaned the blood off his blade and sheathed the weapon. He squatted down to examine the corpse.

In death, the man's poor condition was even more apparent. He was skin and bone, wasted away from malnourishment. Many of his teeth were missing, and no comb had touched hair or beard for months. Tomas sniffed once and cringed. No soap had touched his skin, either. Dried blood caked around his mouth and in his beard.

Tomas chewed on his lower lip as he thought.

This didn't sit right.

But he couldn't put his finger on why.

He stood up. The body had no more secrets to reveal.

"Tomas?"

He'd been so distracted by the body he hadn't even noticed Elzeth. The sagani still burned. He frowned. "What's wrong?"

"I'm finding it difficult to rest."

"What?"

"I want to rest, but I can't." Elzeth paused. "There's something calling to me."

A colorful series of curses danced across Tomas' thoughts. He couldn't help but look down at the host he'd just killed.

Someday, that would be his future. It was inevitable.

But that day would come much sooner than he hoped if Elzeth couldn't be calmed.

The girl needed his help, though. Whatever danger she was in, it was greater than he'd first thought. And it had been bad enough to begin. "Time to make a choice, partner," Tomas said.

"What choice?"

"The girl first, or you?"

Elzeth was silent for several long seconds. "Me."

Tomas couldn't read Elzeth's mind, if the term even applied in their relationship. But he could feel Elzeth's emotions, which amounted to about the same. Like a couple that had been together for decades, when he combined context with the emotions he felt through their connection, he could usually guess what Elzeth thought. They had no secrets from one another. It was impossible.

Elzeth wanted to help the girl, but didn't think she still lived. And, like Tomas, he saw the decapitated man as a sign of their future.

Tomas considered the problem for a few moments. He wanted to help the girl, too, but he shared Elzeth's view of her odds. It was tragic, but it was the world they lived in.

He had to help himself before he could help others.

He didn't have to say anything. Elzeth could feel his emotions just as Tomas could feel the sagani's.

Tomas walked away from the dead host. He found a spot with tall grass and a bush that would protect him from view. He sat down cross-legged and closed his eyes.

Elzeth still burned brightly, as though they were in the midst of heated combat.

Tomas focused on his breath. In and out through the nose, slow and even. At first, his body demanded more air, but Tomas didn't relent.

Deprived of the fuel it required, Elzeth's fire stopped growing. The barrier between them solidified as the heat faded.

Tomas worked his way from the top of his head down. He relaxed the muscles in his face, then his tongue, then his shoulders. Muscle by muscle, he assumed a state of ease.

Again, his body fought. When Elzeth burned within him, his desire was to run, to jump, and to fight. He wanted to move. He had to move.

Tomas respected the wisdom of his body, but in this case, the mind knew better. Slowly, it asserted its dominance.

Tomas didn't know why the technique worked. Its purpose hadn't been this. He'd learned it in the sword school he'd grown up in as a method of meditation.

But it worked, and for now, that was enough. As the muscles in his body relaxed, Elzeth's flame dimmed. It became a loop. The more he relaxed, the greater control Elzeth could assert over his power. As the flame sputtered out, Tomas found it easier to relax.

Before long, Tomas was completely relaxed, and Elzeth was at ease. "Good?" Tomas asked.

"Yes. Thank you." Elzeth hesitated. "But I'm going to restrain myself. Only for absolute necessity, until we have a better idea what's happening."

Tomas looked up at the mountain. "You said you heard something?"

"I did. At the edge of my understanding. I think Tatum might have been right about this mountain."

Tomas grunted. Perhaps he should have gone south. Maybe it was worth listening to a local when they warned you from a place. A lesson for another day, he supposed.

He returned to where the girl had slept. He found her tracks, still heading west, easily enough.

It was time to find out what had happened to her.

5

Tomas followed the tracks.

The trail wasn't hard to follow. The girl had kept close to the stream. Broken twigs, muddy footsteps, and trampled grass all provided clues. Her pace had slowed from the day before. Her footsteps were closer together. Often, he saw clusters of footsteps as she stopped and rested. She grew weaker with every hour.

Tomas still couldn't explain her direction. Why up? Why farther away from Tatum's house?

If she'd traveled west for a bit, he might have understood. Eventually, though, she should have doubled back. Reason should have reasserted itself.

Eventually, the tracks broke away from the stream. But when they did, they only climbed higher into the mountains. The girl seemed determined to travel as far away from help as possible.

It gave Tomas pause.

The girl's actions weren't rational. By itself, that didn't bother him. Tatum had called her a young girl, so Tomas assumed she was maybe nine or ten. She'd seen her father die, and she was alone in a land all too happy to kill her. Few, if any, of her choices would be rational. But he still expected her to at least travel downhill. Humans, by nature, took the easy path. Especially when they were frightened.

Between the girl, the mad host, and Elzeth, Tomas was beginning to feel particularly uneasy. The girl was most likely dead, and if he was reasonable, he'd turn around.

He'd come this far, though. Doubt would haunt him unless he at least found the body.

The trail became more difficult to follow. The ground away from the stream was dry and hard, meaning there were few footprints to find. Several times, he had to guess which way she had traveled. A difficult task, considering she followed no reason Tomas understood.

Eventually, though, the girl's trail intersected a well-worn game trail. One print, clear as day, reassured Tomas he was on the right path. Tomas picked up the pace, feeling the soreness in the back of his legs as he continued to climb higher.

Another sagani, this one shaped like an oversized coyote, waited near a bend in the trail. It sat on its hind legs, its gaze locked on Tomas.

Tomas slowed. A wise man didn't attack sagani, especially if one was looking right at you. Whatever shape they assumed, they were faster and stronger than they appeared. The only smart way to hunt the creatures was hidden, with at least a hundred yards separating you and it, and a rifle in hand.

Tomas was zero for three.

For a time, he wondered if he might have to work his way around the creature. The sagani seemed in no hurry to move, and Tomas felt a growing urge to get off this mountain as quickly as possible.

A few moments before he broke, the sagani stood up on all fours and trotted away, casting glances back at Tomas.

He hurried.

The game trail continued to ascend. It turned north, which put the mountains on his left. The ground on his right started to slope away, becoming steeper and steeper. Before long, Tomas found himself walking along the edge of a ledge that dropped twenty feet or so. Not enough to hurt him, but worth being wary of.

Shen crawled over the crest of the horizon to his right, adding more light to the scene.

A high-pitched scream came from somewhere up ahead.

The sort of scream that might have come from a young girl.

Tomas ran.

Elzeth remained stubbornly silent, which worried Tomas. It was unlike Elzeth not to help. Tomas trusted Elzeth would aid him if his own life was in danger, but he worried Elzeth might not move a muscle for the girl. Their experience had shaken the sagani more than Tomas expected.

Any exhaustion he felt vanished when the girl screamed again, closer this time. Another sound followed the scream, too quiet for Tomas to understand. She wasn't alone. He ran as fast as his legs could carry him, the drop to his right forgotten.

Ahead, the path bent to the left. The rising elevation of the foothills blocked Tomas' view of what lay beyond the bend. When he reached the corner, he finally found the girl.

She was perhaps a hundred feet beyond the bend. She wasn't as small as he expected, but he couldn't guess her age. It was hard to tell in the dark from this distance. She stood near the edge of the ledge, which had grown to thirty feet tall. She'd been trapped there by two men, each brandishing a knife.

The men looked like they could be brothers of the man Tomas had killed earlier. Not because they shared blood, but because of the state of their bodies and clothing. Both were too thin, with matted hair and tangled beards. One shuddered uncontrollably, an event that started in the man's knife hand and rippled outward until his whole body seized up. From start to finish, it had lasted less than a heartbeat.

It shouldn't have been possible.

Tomas swore, the sight all too familiar. "Elzeth?"

"I noticed."

"And?"

"Only if necessary."

Tomas would have sworn again, but the fear in Elzeth's tone quenched his anger. It wasn't like the sagani to be terrified.

One of the men was close to the girl, herding her ever closer to the edge. The other watched the path. The one watching saw Tomas and grunted something, catching the attention of the one close to the girl.

Tomas stopped ten paces from the man guarding the road. Without Elzeth, he wasn't fast enough to kill them both before they hurt the girl. He spread his arms out wide, far away from his sword. "Let the girl go."

As their attention focused on him, Tomas got his first clear look at the girl. She seemed older than he expected. Scared as she was, though, he saw her eyes taking in the situation, looking for a way out.

The man closest to him tilted his head, the bones in his neck cracking as he craned it to an uncomfortable angle. Like the man down below, the madness had completely taken him. Tomas doubted he could even hear any words Tomas said.

The other one, though, still had some semblance of sanity left. He blinked, his eyes briefly focusing on Tomas before once again staring into nothingness. "It wants the girl. She's young."

"What? Who?"

But there was no answer. Both men stared at a mountain behind Tomas. They stared so hard Tomas risked a glance back, but there was nothing to see. Just a silent mountain, outlined by Tolkin as it fell from the night sky.

Tomas raised his voice, hoping he could penetrate their thoughts once more. "Let the girl go! She's done you no harm."

He took a cautious step forward.

The one closest to the girl snapped his head around, reminding Tomas of the host he'd killed earlier. With one quick motion, he pushed the girl off the ledge.

Her scream died when she hit the bottom.

6

Tomas drew his sword. The man closest to him cocked his head, as though listening to an order only he could hear. The man frowned, and his eyes focused on Tomas once again. "What are you?" he asked.

When he received no answer, he threatened Tomas with his knife. "Come with us."

Tomas noted the man's grip on his weapon. He had no training.

"Come with us," the man repeated. Behind him, the one who had pushed the girl off the ledge turned to face Tomas. He, too, held up his knife. Both hosts moved in perfect unison, as though they shared a mind.

Elzeth refused to stir.

Tomas moved toward the closer of the men, sword leveled before him. He didn't like the idea of facing both hosts at the same time.

Both men continued to wave their knives, but neither moved in response to Tomas' advance. As Tomas neared, he saw tears staining the cheek of the man nearest him. The sight brought Tomas to a stop.

The man's eyes focused for a moment, and for the first time, Tomas felt as though he was looking at the man. Not the being the sagani had transformed him into.

His enemy dropped his knife and spread his arms out wide. He grimaced and his arms quivered as though he was holding enormous weights. He looked Tomas in the eye. "Kill me. Please."

Tomas did.

One cut, clean through the throat.

The man died with a smile on his face, a triumphant grin aimed at an enemy Tomas couldn't see.

The second man reacted. He charged, knife pointed at Tomas' heart. He ran faster than any human should, closing the space between them in a second.

Fast as he was, he couldn't outrun Tomas' sword. Tomas cut as he moved, and the outstretched knife hand was separated from its owner. The weapon, still tightly clutched in the dead hand, embedded in the dirt.

The loss of the hand didn't bother the man in the least. He spun, spraying blood in all directions, and snarled. He leaped at Tomas like a wolf, jaws open wide, aimed at Tomas' neck. Tomas stabbed out, the tip of his sword entering the man's mouth and then out the back of his skull.

It should have killed the man, but he still struggled. Tomas twisted and snapped the blade down and across. The motion flung the man to the ground.

He refused to die.

Tomas took a few steps back, not out of fear, but of caution. He knew the speed of the host, and nothing was more dangerous than a man on the brink of death. He had nothing left to lose.

The man awkwardly took a stance on all fours. Tomas grimaced as he saw the man put weight on the bloody stump where his hand had once been. The man snarled, again acting as more wolf than man.

He shuffled toward Tomas, who retreated a few more steps.

Finally, the man's body realized it was supposed to be dead. He collapsed to the ground, twitched a few times, and was still.

Tomas watched for a full minute before stepping forward and taking the man's head. With a host, it always paid to be sure.

He looked around at the scene. He shuddered.

The cost of becoming a host was something he'd lived with for many years now. He didn't fear death, because he should have died long ago. The gate would welcome him in time.

But not like this.

Not when everything had been stripped from him. Not when he became something less than human.

He hoped someone killed him before it came to that. If not, he might just kill himself. Better that than this.

He shuddered again, both of his most recent kills worming under his skin. Violence was a part of life. But he didn't like being reminded of the future that awaited him.

"We should leave," Elzeth said.

The comment, barely louder than a whisper, brought Tomas back to the present. He nodded absently. Curiosity demanded he remain, but some risks were too great, even for him. The girl's death was tragic, but it broke the only chain that tied him to the mountain.

He looked up at the peaks. Some mysteries were better left unsolved.

He walked to the edge of the ledge and glanced over. The girl was down there, her limbs at an unnatural angle.

It was a shame. He didn't know the girl, but any child deserved better than this.

He took a knee and spoke softly into the night.

FROM THE ONE we became many;
To the One we return.
May the gates beyond
Welcome your weary soul.

THEN HE STOOD. He took one last look at the girl. Hopefully her soul found something better in whatever came next.

She blinked.

Tomas jumped and swore.

He had little doubt she was dying, but somehow, she still lived. For a moment, he was torn by indecision. Had she been in the service with him, or an animal, he would have ended her misery. They were miles from help.

But she was a girl, and she still drew breath. He had to at least try.

"Elzeth?"

There was no response. Perhaps he could force Elzeth to wake by jumping, but he didn't want to trust his life to Elzeth's mood. He searched for a way down to the girl, but no easy routes presented themselves. He'd have to backtrack and come at the area from a different direction. By the time he did that, she'd be gone.

Then he saw the sagani. It slithered like a snake across the loose rock at the bottom of the ledge. It approached the girl without a hint of caution.

"Elzeth?"

"I see it."

"What's it doing?"

"Either saving her life or killing her."

Tomas' heart beat faster. "We should get down there!"

"No."

Tomas considered jumping again. If Elzeth wanted to live, he'd have to help.

But there were no guarantees. And the girl was dying. It wasn't like he would be any better help.

The sagani curled around the girl. It made no attempt to harm her, which meant only one thing.

He'd been in a similar situation once, his blood pouring out into the snow. He had some idea of what the girl experienced. Her mind would be filled with the unspoken communion with the sagani. Ultimately, it would be her choice.

But she was too young to have to make such a choice. She couldn't begin to fathom the consequences.

Tomas could do nothing but watch.

The sagani began to glow. A pale red at first, reminding Tomas of Tolkin's light. But then it brightened and turned white. Tomas shielded his eyes. The girl's decision had been made.

He'd never seen the process from the outside.

There was little to see.

The sagani burned brighter and brighter, and then there was one soundless, blinding flash of light.

When Tomas' sight returned, the sagani was gone.

7

Tomas watched the small fire as the wood crackled and popped. The wood had been wetter than he would have liked, and it released a quiet, constant medley of sound as the flames consumed it. The noise didn't bother the sleeping girl, though he wasn't sure much would.

He stared into the fire, mind blank, exhausted but unable to sleep.

They were still in the mountains, although lower than the ledge where he'd first seen her. His arms ached from carrying her. With Elzeth, the task would have been easy, but the sagani hadn't even considered it.

He'd set what bones he could, and the rest was out of his hands. She lived or died on her own.

The flames danced in his vision, strangely hypnotic.

Elzeth disturbed his peace. "We need to talk."

"Then talk."

"We should leave this place."

"Soon as the girl's healed enough to move, we'll make our way back to Tatum's home."

"Now."

Tomas leaned back and looked up to the stars. "If you would have helped, we might have been able to save her."

They'd argued plenty over the years, but Tomas didn't remember ever being quite this angry with his partner. Never before did they seem as different as they did today.

"If I helped, there's a good chance you'd be as mad as those prospectors. Uglier, too."

Elzeth's attempt at humor landed flat. Tomas might have helped the girl. Elzeth had denied him the chance. A small shooting star streaked across the sky. For a brief moment, it burned bright, then vanished. "Is it really that bad?"

"It is."

Tomas closed his eyes. Despite the temptation, he couldn't call Elzeth a coward. They'd faced death and worse too often. The sagani tended more toward caution, but was more than willing to put his life on the line when the moment demanded it.

He opened his eyes. He didn't know much about kids, but she looked older than he'd first guessed. Twelve, maybe? He couldn't say. She wasn't very tall, but her face didn't look young. Underneath the grime of the road and the dried blood from her injuries, he suspected she had light hair. The cuts he'd noticed when he first found her were already healed, and if he guessed right, she'd be fit to walk soon.

She was burning fast.

"She doesn't deserve this," Tomas said.

"Not for us to say," Elzeth replied. "She'll live now, at least for a while. Isn't that something?"

"She keeps burning like that, it won't be long. Death might have been a mercy."

He watched her rest for a while.

"You didn't give me an answer," Elzeth said.

"We're not leaving her here alone."

Elzeth went silent.

"What frightens you so?" Tomas asked.

"I had no control," Elzeth said.

That didn't seem frightening enough to justify abandoning a girl to her fate. Tomas didn't say anything, but Elzeth sensed his emotion well enough.

"Imagine swinging your sword but not knowing where it would cut," the sagani said. "Actually, it's even worse. Imagine you have to swing your sword, but someone else decides where the strike lands. How eager would you be to draw your blade then?"

Tomas poked at the fire with a long stick, rearranging the burning branches so they would catch more evenly. He added a bit more wood to the fire. There was no real need for the flame. He'd be warm enough without it, and the girl even more so. He just wanted to drive away the darkness for what remained of the evening. "Something's causing this?"

"Feels that way."

"Any ideas who or what?"

"No. Never felt anything like it."

Tomas grunted. "We wait for her to heal. Then we'll take her down, and we won't return." A very small part of him was curious, but if the mountain worried Elzeth this much, caution was warranted. He felt Elzeth's rumble of discontent, but he refused to simply abandon the girl. Some sins couldn't be washed away, no matter how long one atoned for them.

"She's not right," Elzeth said.

"Is it because of her age?" Tomas had never met a host so young.

"No." Elzeth paused. "I can't describe it. She's like no host we've ever come across."

Off in the distance, Tomas caught the first hints of the

morning light on the horizon. He would have no answers anytime soon. And his decision wouldn't change. "You keeping watch?"

"Of course."

Tomas rearranged the fire one last time, added the last of the wood he'd gathered, then lay down and closed his eyes. It took a few minutes, but eventually sleep took him.

He awoke to a scream.

He shot upright, eyes open, hand on the hilt of his sword. But he saw no threat. Their camp was empty except for him and the girl.

But she was sitting tall, her eyes wide. They were bright blue, and for a moment, Tomas swore that they shone. Her stare pierced him, but when he shifted his position, her gaze never moved. He glanced behind him, but there was nothing there. Like the hosts he'd encountered earlier, she was staring at something he couldn't see.

She screamed again, the pitch much lower than he expected from such a small girl.

"Elzeth?" he asked.

"No idea," came the immediate reply. "One moment she was resting, the next she's like this. Is this normal for human children?"

Tomas scrambled over to the girl. Her scream died, but she continued to stare into the distance. The sudden silence seemed to be more a pause than a cessation. Tentatively, he reached out toward her shoulder.

She screamed again, and he winced against the assault on his ears. He grabbed for her shoulder, and the scream cut off as soon as he touched her. For the briefest of moments, he feared that he had harmed her.

She turned her head toward him and blinked. Her eyes

met his, and he believed she saw him now, for the first time. "It's here," she said.

"Who?" Tomas asked.

But the girl's eyes rolled up in her head and she fell backward. Tomas caught her as she fell and laid her to rest gently. Within moments, her breathing was deep and even. His own heart pounded far faster than hers.

"Hells," he said.

While he'd slept, dawn had broken. The sun warmed the wide clearing he'd found last night, but it couldn't banish the chill that settled in his bones.

"I still think we should leave," Elzeth said.

Tomas was beginning to think the sagani made a lot of sense.

8

D espite the disturbance, the girl didn't seem to be in any rush to wake up again. She snored softly while Tomas kept watch.

He turned over the questions this mountain raised, examining what he knew from different angles, but nothing made sense. Tatum's warnings echoed ominously in his memories. This mountain *was* crawling with sagani, and though Tomas wasn't ready to call them evil, they weren't like the others he'd crossed paths with over the years. There was something different about them he couldn't quite place.

The girl wasn't going to wake any time soon. If anything, her snoring grew deeper and louder.

He envied her slumber. His own eyes felt heavy, but returning to sleep was out of the question.

He pulled some food out of his pack and began to eat. He always traveled light, and while Godiva had generously resupplied him, it wouldn't be long before he needed to hunt something down.

Maybe not on this mountain, though. He hadn't seen

any game, which was just one more unusual fact he had no explanation for.

The sun warmed him as it rose. Patchy clouds blew in from the west, journeying from unknown lands to the homes of humanity. A slight breeze, picking up cold air from the top of the mountains, prevented him from becoming too warm.

From their current position, Tomas couldn't even see the speck of Tatum's house. They were completely alone in the world.

He was so close to what he sought, and yet peace felt as elusive as ever.

Tomas lay back in the grass. If not for Elzeth, the girl, and the mysteries of the mountain, he'd call this a perfect moment.

Someday, soon, he'd find a place where he could truly rest. Where he could leave behind the troubles of the world.

The girl woke less than an hour later, sitting up suddenly. This time, fortunately, the waking wasn't accompanied by an ear-splitting scream.

"Morning," Tomas said. He glanced in the direction of the sun. "Or maybe afternoon."

The girl stared at him with a look that somehow didn't seem appropriate on one so young. Now that she was awake, Tomas revised his estimate of her age upward. He'd met others like her before, mostly during the war. Children whose childhood had been stolen from them, thrusting them into an uncaring world of adults before their time.

He saw hard-earned wisdom in the girl's eyes.

She didn't shout when she saw him. Nor did she embrace him like a child seeking protection. She studied him, wary.

He knew she wore a knife near her right hip. The sheath

had poked into his chest as he'd carried her the night before. He hadn't taken it, and he saw her discreetly brush her hand across her side to ensure it was still there.

"Name's Tomas," he said.

She didn't respond for almost a full minute, but he figured they were in no particular rush. "Lyana," she said.

"Hungry?" Tomas held up some of his food.

She nodded quickly, and he tossed his pack over to her. "Help yourself to as much as you want."

She snatched his pack out of the air and rummaged through it. She pulled out enough for two meals and then looked up. "Truly?"

It looked like the need for a hunting trip had just grown. He nodded.

She tore into the food and was several bites in before she remembered her manners. "Thank you."

"You're welcome." He tossed her his water skin, which she also caught with ease. Her reaction had started as soon as he'd moved.

"She's burning real hot," Elzeth said.

Tomas had suspected the same. It wasn't unusual. A host was always born on the edge of a person's death. The first challenge a host had to overcome was a body's injuries, and Lyana had been hurt badly. The fact she was sitting up and eating was a wonder in itself. "Give her time," Tomas replied.

It didn't take Lyana long to eat through half of Tomas' remaining food. Then she burped and leaned back. "I don't feel right."

"How much do you remember of last night?"

"Those men were chasing me," she said, no trace of fear in her voice. "One pushed me, and then I woke up here."

Tomas scratched at the back of his neck. He'd never had

to explain this to anyone, much less a child. "Do you know what a host is?"

She stared at him as though he were stupid. "I'm fourteen. Of course I know what a host is."

"Well, you are one now."

She sat up straight at that. Then she looked down at her hands, flexing them into fists, then relaxing them. She examined her hands for the better part of a minute. Without any warning, she made a fist with her left hand and slammed it into the ground.

Without Elzeth's aid, Tomas only saw a blur of motion. Dirt and clumps of clay flew in all directions, and Tomas raised a hand to shield his face.

When the dust settled, Lyana was again staring at her hand. A new, small crater now existed near her left leg.

Finally, she tore her gaze away from her hand. She fixed it on him. "Give me your sword."

"Excuse me?" He wasn't sure he'd heard correctly.

Lyana was on her feet almost faster than he could follow. Elzeth rumbled to life. Tomas held up his hands, not quite sure what Lyana intended.

"Give me your sword," she repeated. It was beginning to sound an awful lot like a threat.

He stood, slowly, keeping his hands up to communicate that he meant no harm. For a heartbeat, he wondered if she might want his sword for some other type of test.

He dismissed the idea almost as quickly as it came to him. She still had the knife. Any test with a weapon would be easier with that.

And she wasn't asking in a manner that made him think she was going to return it.

Did she mean him harm? "I'm not one to give away my sword. We've been through a lot together. The answer is no."

She tensed, and Tomas came within a breath of drawing his weapon.

Against anyone else, he would have. But he had no desire to draw against a fourteen-year-old girl.

"I don't mean to attack you," Lyana said. "You've done me a kindness by taking care of me and feeding me. You have my gratitude. But I will have that sword."

Tomas' eyes darted around, looking for something that ended this standoff and didn't require violence. "Why?" he asked, stalling for time.

"Because," she said, "I know the man who killed my father, and I mean to kill him myself."

9

L yana didn't give him a chance to respond. She lunged for him, arm outstretched, hand grasping for his sword.

She was quick. Faster than she had any right to be, even as a host. She covered the five paces between them in less than a heartbeat.

Tomas twisted away.

For all her speed, she had no skill or training. The way she shifted her body, she might as well have announced her intent loudly before charging.

Her speed was still almost enough. Had she started just a step or two closer, she might have gotten her hand on his sword. She ran past him, sliding to a stop in the grass a dozen paces behind him. She looked down at her feet as though she wasn't sure how she'd gotten there.

He turned to face her. "I don't want to fight."

"Then give me your sword."

"No."

She ran at him again. This time she controlled her speed. She was still faster than any human could dream of, but slower than her first charge. She learned quickly from her failures.

In a way, being reborn as a host was like waking up in an entirely new body. Tomas had needed days to learn both his abilities and limits. For all the years he'd been a host, he still hadn't mastered the strength Elzeth provided.

Still, Tomas had no challenge deciphering her intent. The space between them gave him another second to prepare. He grimaced as he threw his fist into her stomach. It connected, driving the wind from her lungs.

As she stumbled, arms wrapped around her stomach, Tomas retreated. Burning as hot as she was, she probably barely felt the hit, but that didn't make him feel any better about it.

For a brief moment, he considered just giving her the weapon. He'd relied on his sword through the war and the adventures that had followed him after. When all else had been lost, it had been sturdy in his hand. But it was still just a piece of sharpened steel.

He came to his senses. If he gave her his sword, he would be condoning her outlandish revenge scheme. Host or not, she was still a girl, alone on the frontier. She needed help, not a sword.

She shook off the hit, and once again he held up his hands. "I want to help."

Lyana growled, and a shudder ran through her body.

Tomas frowned. A tic? The girl hadn't even been a host for a full day yet.

She rushed at him again, but she seemed to have forgotten the lessons she'd just learned. Her charge was all speed and anger, without even a hint of control.

Tomas laid her flat with a single punch. She collapsed like a rag doll, and he looked down at her, sprawled in the grass. He barely knew her, but that last attack had been different than the first.

"She's not going to be out long, burning like that," Elzeth observed.

Tomas agreed. He stepped back and waited.

He wasn't proud to admit it, but he considered walking away. This was already far more trouble than he'd hoped for, and he got the foreboding sense that if he stuck around, the girl would lead him into far worse.

Lyana didn't keep him waiting long. She blinked her eyes and looked around, as though she wasn't sure where she was. She sat up and rubbed at her head. "Sorry," she said. "I'm not sure what came over me."

Tomas didn't step any closer, but he did squat down to her level. "It's a lot to take in. But you're using too much of your strength. Will you let me help you?"

She squeezed her eyes shut and pulled at the roots of the grass. Her shoulders rose until they were almost covering her ears. Tomas tensed. If this was the madness, he'd never seen anything quite like it.

Nothing on this mountain behaved the way he expected. If he wasn't careful, soon the trees would be singing lulla-bies and the hares would jump obediently into a pot of stew. Though that last one might prove useful soon.

Lyana took a deep breath, and then another. Her shoul-ders fell first, and then her white-knuckle grip on the roots of the grass relaxed. Finally, she opened her eyes. She'd fought a battle with herself and won this round.

"I'm sorry," she said again. "It's just...every time I think about Pa, I think about taking your sword..." She squeezed her eyes closed again and visibly struggled to master herself. "It's like I lose control. It's all I can think about."

What she described was unlike the signs of madness

Tomas understood. But she shouldn't have any signs of madness anyway. It was far too early.

Something else was happening.

Fear flashed in her eyes, and he thought of what Elzeth had said the night before about losing control.

"The first thing we need to do is help you master your strength," Tomas said. "I think it will help."

She gritted her teeth. "Please."

"Focus on your breath," Tomas began. "Breathe through your nose. Count to four as you breathe in, then count to six as you breathe out."

She counted out loud, and Tomas almost corrected her, but he held his tongue. He let her repeat a few cycles, then continued. "Once you've done that, I want you to go down through your body. Start at the very top of your head and relax every muscle. Loosen your jaw. Relax your tongue. Drop your shoulders." He spoke slowly, only issuing each instruction once he was sure the previous one had been followed.

It appeared to be working. Her breath became even and her body stilled.

He gave her a bit longer, then decided it was time for the test. Focused meditation was all well and good, but it didn't do much good for day-to-day living. "Try opening your eyes."

"I don't want to."

"You'll be fine. You're doing great."

She cracked open one eye, peeking through her eyelashes as though expecting to see a monster. Then she worked up the courage to open the eye completely. Soon both were open and she offered him a hesitant smile. "I don't feel it anymore."

"It's still there," Tomas said. "It will be for the rest of

your life."

She looked to be near the verge of tears, but was too proud to let any of them fall. "How does it work?"

"Nobody knows for sure. It's a little different for everyone, I reckon. It'll respond when you need help. You'll heal faster. You'll be stronger and quicker than most anyone." He paused. "And I think, once you're off this mountain, it'll be easier to control."

Lyana looked down at her hands again. "Stronger and faster?"

Tomas knew where that particular train of thought led. "It's a dangerous gift," he said. "The more you use it, the closer you become to those men who were after you."

The mention of the men was a mistake. He knew it the moment it left his lips, but there was no taking it back.

"Give me your sword," she said.

He heard her focusing on her breath. She remained in control. For now.

"No."

"Those men killed my father. They deserve justice."

"They deserve death, but they'll travel to the gate soon enough. Death always follows close behind the madness. No need for you to go after them."

"I want to kill them."

"I hear you. But I intend to take you down to the last house you passed. The man who lives there is a doctor. He can make sure you're well. Then we can take you to the nearest village, see if there's anyone who can take you in."

"I won't go. I mean to see justice done." She studied him, and he caught the fierce intelligence in her gaze. She might be fourteen, but he suspected it would be a mistake to underestimate her. "Perhaps you might be persuaded to join me. My father carried his life savings in his pack.

Help me, then we can return to the camp and it will be yours."

Tomas smiled. "I've already been through your camp. There was very little of value. But it was a nice try."

Lyana changed tactics. "Would you leave me here, all alone?"

"Won't you leave with me? Tatum and his family seemed kind enough."

"You'd have to force me."

He'd been lying. He didn't have a trump card in his hand, and she knew the score. She'd called his bluff. He didn't want to leave her alone, but he also wasn't willing to physically force her to safety.

Too clever for her own good.

He tried one last suggestion. "Being a host means a short life for most. I can teach you how to live longer. I've found the secret."

She stared at him, expressionless. "Not interested."

Tomas grimaced. "A compromise, then. We stay here one more day. You can heal, and I can rest. Tomorrow, we'll see if your mind has changed."

She stood. "I have a better idea. I'll leave, and you do whatever you think is best." She gave him a short bow. "Thank you for your help."

Lyana turned on her heel and started up the mountain.

Tomas sat there, watching.

"Are all human children like that?" Elzeth asked.

"I don't have a lot of experience," Tomas replied, "but I hope not."

10

Tomas lay back in the grass and watched the clouds drift by. It didn't take Elzeth long to comment.

"You going after her?"

"Hoping she changes her mind when she realizes I'm not going to follow."

Elzeth chuckled.

"She might come back," Tomas objected.

"That's every bit as likely as you getting elected deacon of the local church."

"It's possible," Tomas argued. "Just you wait."

Twenty minutes passed.

An hour.

Tomas stretched and sat up. "She's not coming back, is she?"

Elzeth gloated in silence.

"No need to rub it in." Tomas looked around for any sign of Lyana, but he'd watched the girl leave and hadn't seen any movement since. He sighed. "We should have turned south."

"You'll learn one of these days," Elzeth said.

"Thoughts?"

"I want nothing to do with any of it," Elzeth answered. "If she wants to go get herself killed, it's all the same to me."

"Admit it, you'd feel bad."

"A state I much prefer to being dead."

Tomas let his gaze travel higher up the mountain. Somehow, it seemed even more dangerous in the light of day. "I get the feeling that if we follow, you aren't going to have the choice to remain slumbering much longer. I'll need you."

"I was thinking the same."

The wind gusted from the peaks, sending a sudden chill down Tomas' spine. He wasn't sure why he'd ever considered the look of those peaks majestic. The closer he came, the more they loomed over him.

"Practice?" Tomas asked.

He sensed Elzeth's agreement.

He took a deep breath and Elzeth stirred to life inside him.

Then he erupted in an inferno of power.

The force of it nearly stole Tomas' breath away. Strength flooded his limbs, and when he looked back to the peaks, he felt foolish for having once feared them. He felt drawn to them like steel to a magnet. With Elzeth burning so bright, he could be there before the sun set.

The barriers that separated Tomas and Elzeth began to fray, withering at the edges from Elzeth's intense heat. There was a promise there. If Tomas let the barrier dissolve, he'd become stronger and faster than any enemy.

He'd be whole.

He refused the offer. Tomas clutched the barrier tightly in his mind, the way a toddler clung to their favorite blanket.

The cost of unity was sanity.

Elzeth dimmed, and as he did, so did Tomas' desires. Both the strength of unity and the mountains no longer held their appeal.

"What was that?" Tomas asked.

"What I've been struggling against since we got here. I've never wanted unity so badly. The more awake I am, the worse it is."

Tomas had a sense of it. Elzeth's distress lent his own body a nervous energy, and he succumbed to the need to pace back and forth to burn it off. "I didn't know it was so strong. Sorry."

Elzeth accepted the apology. "Doesn't answer the question, though."

It didn't. "Can you fight it?"

Elzeth didn't answer for a long time.

Lyana needed the answer to be yes. If not, Tomas wasn't any good to her. But that power was unsustainable. The burden largely fell on Elzeth to manage.

Finding the right balance had taken them years, and they could ill afford to lose it.

Eventually, the strength faded from his limbs, and he felt human once again. When Elzeth answered, he sounded exhausted. "I think so. It's tiring, though. Fighting the temptation while keeping focused is twice as hard."

Tomas sat down, giving Elzeth time to rest.

"It's like when we've been alone for a few months and you come across a woman you find attractive," Elzeth said.

The corner of Tomas' mouth turned up in a smile. When he'd first become a host, his intimate life had suffered. It had taken a long time to come to terms with the fact he'd never truly be alone again.

That shame had gone. He knew it disturbed most women, but it was easy enough for him to pass as simply human. He told very few people that he was a host, and this was just one reason.

Then he frowned. He looked up at the mountains, which once again loomed over him, threatening the sky with their sharp ridges. "Can you try again?"

Elzeth awakened again. This time, the transition was less dramatic than before. He still burned too fast at first, then faded to a more comfortable level.

Tomas raised his eyes to the mountains one last time. The wind passing over them and rushing down the side sounded like a song, one he wanted to hear more clearly. Tomas closed his eyes and listened, and almost stood up and started walking higher.

He thought of Lyana. He was still concerned about her. She was out there, seeking revenge against the man who had killed her father.

He wanted to kill the man and his comrades, too. More than he'd wanted to kill anything in a long time. They'd left a young girl alone on a mountain that was sure to kill her. They deserved a slow and painful death. The guilty man was up there with his friends, waiting for them, unsuspecting. And Tomas knew where he was. It appeared before him, so vivid he swore it was real. "That's enough," Tomas said.

Elzeth relaxed, falling quickly into his near-slumber.

The vision disappeared, but it left Tomas shaken. He turned his attention to Elzeth. "How was it?"

"Better," Elzeth said. "If I can assert control over the transition, I can recover well. I might recommend not getting surprised, though. It might take me a bit to regain control, and if you're fighting, it'll be even harder."

Tomas stared at the peaks. He didn't want to go up there

at all. Nor did he have any desire to kill the stranger he'd just seen.

He began packing again, the pack almost empty. He'd offered his food to Lyana expecting a quick return to Tatum's house. Now he only had enough to survive a few more days. Unfortunately, it was a challenge he didn't have time to solve right now.

He shouldered the pack with a sigh. Problems never visited him alone. They always came with friends, uninvited guests in his life.

"We're doing this?" Elzeth asked.

Tomas had an unexpected memory of a friend from childhood. Kaius and he had been close in the sword school that had raised Tomas. The two of them delighted in making life difficult for the instructors.

They'd always had an uncanny ability to push one another to do things neither would have considered alone. Neither wanted to be the one to say no.

"What was that?" Elzeth sensed the emotion, but not the thought behind it.

"An old friend I hadn't thought about in ages," Tomas said. "I was reminded of our friendship just now."

"Would he have also called this task foolish?"

Tomas grinned. "He would have. And he would have been right by my side the entire time. You'd like him."

He cinched the straps on his pack so that it was tight against his back. Then he followed Lyana higher up the mountain.

"She might be hard to track," Elzeth said. "You have any ideas what direction we should begin our search?"

"I can do better," Tomas replied. "I know where she's going."

11

The exertion of hiking up the mountain almost succeeded in washing away Tomas' cares of the world. The smell of pine trees filled his nose. Whenever his path brought him to a viewpoint through the trees, he could see for miles. Despite his hurry, he paused for a moment at those viewpoints to catch his breath and enjoy the view.

He refilled his water skin in a stream, nearly freezing his hand as he submerged it in the icy cold water. The burbling of the stream made him drowsy, so he splashed some of the water on his face and continued on.

Despite the warmth of the day, there were no bugs here. Tomas assumed it was another strange manifestation of whatever was happening on this mountain, but it was one he wasn't going to question.

He summited a small rise, then descended the other side of the hill, losing several hundred feet of elevation. He transitioned across a wide ridge and started climbing higher. After another hour he stumbled across a mountain lake. The water was cold, clear, and inviting. It practically begged him to fashion a pole and cast a line. He settled for resting briefly on its shores, imagining building a house here and settling down.

He could imagine it without much problem.

Maybe this was a place he would be willing to call home someday.

But the mountain never let him forget its presence. The bugs weren't the only animals missing. He found little evidence of wildlife, and the area was as silent a place as he'd ever been. No birds chirped in the trees, and nothing moved in the underbrush. Tranquil as the place may be, it wasn't natural.

He was close to finding his home, but not there yet.

Tomas didn't worry much about tracking Lyana's exact path. He knew where she was heading, and there were only a few ways up the mountain that made sense. He didn't need to follow her, he just needed to reach their destination first.

People had been on these trails recently. Broken twigs and trampled grasses provided plenty of evidence. Too many to be the girl.

It didn't much matter. They were all drawn to the same place.

After another hour, Tomas thought he saw a glint of something a few hundred feet to his left. He glanced and saw a prospector, watching him from far away. Through the trees, Tomas could barely make him out, but he seemed clean shaven, making him an outlier around here.

He watched Tomas for a minute, then turned and disappeared. Tomas considered giving chase but thought better of it. He was looking for Lyana, and she would be higher up.

As he continued, he searched for the prospector again, but he was nowhere to be found.

He entered a particularly thick patch of pine forest, threading his way between the tall, thin trunks.

It was late afternoon when Tomas heard the snap of a twig a ways behind him. He smiled, but continued on as though he hadn't heard. A few minutes later, another twig broke. It was hard to avoid, if one wasn't used to moving carefully.

He walked a little ways farther until he found a nice boulder to sit on. He unslung his pack, took out a bite to eat, and sipped from his water skin.

"Are you trying to get her to attack?" Elzeth asked.

"Just baiting her." She'd stormed off without supplies. He'd be starving if he were in her place. Her body might have healed, but such healing came with a cost she was likely still paying. He glanced in his pack. If his gamble paid off, food would be a serious issue soon. And with nothing to hunt on these slopes, the issue might be a deadly one.

Just another reason to get her off this mountain as fast as possible.

She held out longer than he expected. He ate slowly, ensuring the sights and smells of his food would carry.

Then she revealed herself, emerging from behind a clump of trees.

Tomas held up his water skin as an offering, and she came closer. "You've been following me," she said.

"Not much for letting children run into danger unaccompanied."

She studied him. "You're like me."

"I am."

"So why won't you kill them?"

"Does no good. Killing them won't bring back your pa. It only puts you in danger." He gestured to the peaks looming above them. "And there's something wrong here. Something that affects hosts. The sooner we're off this mountain, the better off we'll be."

"I'm not leaving until they're dead."

Tomas bit back his retort and glared at her. He didn't get upset about much in life. He'd never found much benefit in whining or complaining. But Lyana shattered his calm like it was a thin piece of poorly blown glass.

She stood there, proud and defiant, certain she was right.

No wonder she frustrated him.

He'd been much the same at her age, and the cost he'd paid for whatever wisdom he now possessed was high.

One last time, he considered the idea of just walking away. It seemed this girl really was trying to find ways to get him killed. No need to help her finish the job.

He really enjoyed being alive.

But he wouldn't leave her alone.

He allowed himself to imagine walking away, then pushed it from his mind. "Do I have your word you'll leave once your father's killer is dead?"

"You do."

"Then let's get this over with." He tossed her some food and put the rest in his pack. He led the way.

"How do you know where we're going?" Lyana asked.

"I wish I could explain. You?"

"Same." She pointed to a spot higher up the mountain. "I just know that it's right about there."

"You two are creeping me out," Elzeth said.

"Join the party."

As they walked, Tomas watched Lyana. His own memories of becoming a host were a jumbled mess of scattered, vivid scenes. The first few days of his own evolution had been difficult. Conversations with other hosts revealed similar stories. He wouldn't tell the girl, but he was curious to watch her over the next couple of days.

Lyana seemed remarkably composed, and Tomas wasn't sure what to make of her. The first host he knew of had only appeared about a hundred years ago, and hosts were still uncommon. He'd seen more in the last day than he had in the past six months. Humanity's questions about the sagani far outnumbered their answers. Maybe, because she was so young, the evolution was easier. Her body had already been in the midst of change. Or perhaps this mountain affected the process.

He couldn't begin to guess.

So he didn't.

He noticed, though, that her concentration was divided. Mostly, she paid remarkable attention to her surroundings. Her eyes wandered restlessly, searching both near and far. She displayed all the awareness he'd expect from someone who had spent the past few months traveling the frontier. But then her pace would slow and her gaze would lose its focus. The moments never lasted long, but they came every few minutes.

He almost dismissed it as a tic, but that didn't feel right to him.

The next time he observed it, he asked her.

She looked down at her feet. "It's hard to describe," she admitted. "But it almost sounds like someone is whispering in my ear. Only I can't quite hear what they're saying."

Tomas frowned, but left the topic alone.

"There's no way she's already speaking with the sagani she's hosting," Elzeth said.

Tomas agreed, but had no other answer.

Her next question surprised him. "When you see the place we're going, what does it look like?"

"A clearing in the trees. A camp of about a dozen people."

"Same," she said. She pointed ahead. "So why are we leaving the forest?"

His frown deepened. She was right. The forest thinned out and ended abruptly about two hundred paces ahead of them. And they were getting close to their destination. He felt it, deep in his bones.

They moved slowly as they reached the end of the trees. The land here sloped upward, and just over the crest, Tomas saw a sheer rock face, maybe twenty feet high. Their destination was just beyond the crest, at the bottom of the rock face.

Tomas dropped into a crawl as they neared the crest. Lyana did the same, and they inched silently forward. When he came close to the crest, he slowly lifted his head to see what lay beyond.

Elzeth swore.

Three hosts stood less than fifty feet away, and each one was staring at Tomas.

12

For two long heartbeats, no one moved. It gave Tomas a few precious seconds to study his opponents. They stared in his direction, but he wasn't sure they saw him. At least, they didn't see him the way he saw them. Their eyes seemed focused on something a long ways away. Perhaps even in a different world.

None of the three's faces or scalps had seen a razor in months, and their emaciated bodies looked like they were more than halfway finished with a quest to become a pile of bones. One supported himself using a sword like a cane. The other two both held dull knives. All three weapons were coated in mud and blood.

Tomas got the distinct impression they had been waiting for company. "Wait here while I bring them down," he said. "Then you—"

Lyana scrambled to her feet and charged them.

Tomas swore and reached for her, but she was burning with everything she had. She was halfway to the three hosts before he finished swearing.

Elzeth responded to Tomas' unspoken desire.

Neither of them believed Lyana would last for more than a moment without them.

Tomas forced himself still, Elzeth's earlier warning still echoing in his mind.

The intensity of the energy and aggression that swept through his body caught him by surprise. He tasted blood on his lips, salty and metallic. His stomach rumbled, hungry for flesh. He imagined tearing through the three hosts with sword and knife, leaving entrails spilling from stomachs. The vision was so vivid, he almost believed it real.

Through it all, he breathed. He inhaled through his nose and imagined the fresh mountain air filling his body from crown to toe. Then he exhaled, breathing out the darkness that dwelled in the hidden chambers of his heart.

He was a killer. But he'd never taken such primal pleasure in the death of others.

The hosts responded to Lyana's attack, meeting her charge with one of their own. The older man who used the sword as a cane proved surprisingly quick, running even as his right ankle folded like a piece of paper whenever he put weight on it.

Tomas didn't just want to kill them. He wanted to tear them to shreds, to feel their life bleeding out from between his teeth. They were abominations, no better than mud stuck on the underside of his boot.

Lyana swung her knife at the first host to cross her path. The host made no effort to defend himself. The knife cut into the host's left shoulder, sliced down and across, then finally snapped somewhere around the host's sternum.

The injured host howled and tried to bite Lyana in the neck, even though he carried his own knife in hand.

Lyana jumped, high enough to clear the injured host.

She stomped down as she fell, landing one foot on the host's head.

In the midst of his own struggle, Tomas still found time to be impressed. The girl's foot caved in the host's skull, killing him instantly.

Unfortunately, landing on a dead body as it fell wasn't a recipe for victory in battle. Lyana's foot got stuck, and the corpse brought her down with it. She landed hard, and Tomas heard something snap.

The next host seized the moment, but like his friend, tried to bite Lyana instead of stabbing her. Lyana held him off, her strength temporarily sufficient.

Elzeth calmed, and reason returned to Tomas. His bloodlust cooled. He pushed himself to his feet and joined the battle. He drew his sword and cut in one motion, the edge of his blade passing easily through the neck of the host on top of Lyana.

The final host, the older man with the sword, balanced on his one good leg and swung at Tomas. The cut was fast, swung with all the power of a host near the end of his life. Tomas didn't even try to block or parry. He let the sword pass in front of him, and as the host did a grotesque one-legged spin, he raised his own sword.

"No!" Lyana shouted from behind him.

Tomas held his cut, waiting for a reason.

"He's the one who killed Pa."

Tomas nodded, then cut twice.

The host's hands flopped to the ground, one of them still holding on tightly to the sword. Then Tomas released Elzeth. The less the sagani did, the better. He walked over to a small boulder and sat, content to watch the end.

Lyana extricated her foot from the skull. Tomas winced as he saw her ankle wobble as she stepped on it. But she was burning so hot he doubted she felt a thing. It held her weight as the host charged her. The host tried to club her with its arms, but Tomas saw she had taken the knife from the first host that had attacked.

She drove the knife into the host's eye. They fell together, but only Lyana stood back up. She pulled the knife from the host's eye and pointed it at Tomas. Her gaze whispered of murder.

Elzeth flared to life as Tomas cursed his own foolishness. He'd thought only of minimizing his use of Elzeth. It hadn't occurred to him he needed to defend himself against the girl, too.

A sudden exhaustion hit him, crashing over him like a wave and then smothering him like a thick and heavy blanket.

They'd fought so long. All he wanted was peace, and yet peace proved ever elusive. If he wandered the whole world, he wasn't sure he'd find it. He opened his arms wide, welcoming her knife.

In the back of his mind, someone screamed, but no one was listening.

If there was one place where he might find peace, it was on the other side of the gate. She could send him there as thanks for his help. He wanted her to.

Once again, reason returned as Elzeth gained control over his strength. Lyana stabbed at his heart, and he deflected her arm with his own as he drove an open palm into the side of her head. The blow dazed her, but she kept coming at him with the knife, her intentions fixed. Tomas hit her again, and this time it was enough to knock her out.

He kicked the knife away from her, then reached into his pack and pulled out some leather straps. He wasn't willing to risk his life on the girl's control. Working quickly, he loosely tied her wrists together, then wrapped another strap just below her knees. He barely tied the knots, but they'd slow her down enough if she attacked again.

Then he settled down to wait. He figured it wouldn't be long.

Elzeth burned quietly, also not willing to extinguish himself in Lyana's presence.

The sun was starting to set behind the mountains, but Tomas expected there would be enough light to make it a fair ways back down the mountain. Once Lyana woke up he would help her seize control again, and they could leave this cursed mountain behind for good.

13

Lyana came to only a few minutes after Tomas retreated. When she saw him, she snarled and jumped to her feet. The leather straps arrested her motion, and she fell face-first back to the ground.

Tomas grimaced.

"Breathe," he said. "You can control it."

She bit at him, but for a moment, the madness left her eyes. She looked around, hurting and confused, before her anger flared up again. Teeth bared, she roared as she fought to free herself.

Tomas waited.

For another full minute, Lyana hovered on the edge of sanity. Her limbs twitched and spasmed, straining against the loose restraints. She kicked at the dirt, heedless of the pain from her injured ankle.

Then her breathing slowed. Her body stopped fighting. Her muscles relaxed.

When she opened her eyes again, he saw the same intelligence he'd noted earlier. She was studying and calculating, planning her next move. He approached and finally let Elzeth rest.

Tomas squatted down and untied the straps from her wrists and legs. He returned the materials to his pack and let her choose what happened next.

Lyana pointed to the oldest of the hosts, the man who had carried the sword. "He was the one who killed Pa."

Tomas nodded, his mind already on other problems. With Lyana injured, they had no chance of reaching safety before the sun set. Unfortunately, the best campsite he'd seen in hours was the very place they were currently standing, and it had three more dead people than he preferred to sleep next to.

"How's your ankle?" he asked.

"Hurts," she answered. "But it's also warm."

"Your body is healing. The more you can rest, the quicker it will work."

She looked at her leg as though seeing it for the first time. "Can I heal from anything?"

Tomas began the gruesome task of moving the bodies. "Dead is still dead, even if you're a host. Short of that, I'm not sure anyone knows. I've recovered from much worse. Best not to push your luck, though. You have limits. They're just different."

He pulled each of the intact bodies a few hundred feet from the camp. He did the same for the older man, then came back for the hands. Lyana stared at the sword lying on the ground. "Yours if you want it," Tomas said.

"Really?"

"I've no need of it. Just so long as you don't go trying to put the pointy end through me, I don't care."

She leaned over and grabbed it like a child reaching for a new toy.

The sword was in pitiful condition. Its edge was chipped in several places, and the tip had suffered mightily under its last owner. Tomas suspected none of that mattered much to the girl. It was more a symbol than a weapon. But it still had plenty of bite if someone attacked. She looked up to him. "Will you teach me how to use it?"

Tomas hesitated.

"Only for protection," she said.

"If you can remain in control for the next day or two, I'll consider it."

"One day," she bargained.

He raised an eyebrow. "Two, now, and longer if you argue again."

That brought a smile to her face. "You bargain better than my pa. He never could figure out how to say 'no' to me."

Tomas looked around the campsite before sitting down. Outside of some spilled blood, he decided it would do. Above them, the sky began to darken. He pulled out some food and passed it to her. She looked up at the sky, and he thought he saw her eyes watering. "Care to talk about it?"

She shook her head.

Together, they finished off a large part of what Tomas had left in his pack. Day turned to night and the brightest of the stars began to twinkle. Tomas found a comfortable position and lay down to rest. His eyes were just beginning to fall shut when Lyana spoke.

"This place isn't what I saw."

He'd noted the same, but hadn't thought much of it. He couldn't explain much of what he'd experienced in the last few days.

She couldn't push it aside so easily. "Doesn't it bother you?"

"There's an awful lot about the last few days that's bothered me," he said, "but there's not much point losing sleep over it."

"There were more people, and in a clearing. They had a proper camp, with tents and everything."

Tomas closed his eyes and wished for sleep to take him.

"I want to know what's happening up here," she said.

He rubbed angrily at his eyes and sat up. "You gave your word."

He swore he could see the gears turning in her mind. It reminded him, of all things, of an old general he used to serve under, who stared at maps and troop placements for hours. Then he'd look up, and when he spoke, Tomas always knew the tactical problem was solved. He didn't want any bit of whatever idea Lyana was hatching.

He lay back down. Tomorrow, he'd take the girl back to Tatum's. Then he'd go south. Find another pristine lake in the mountains, build a home, and forget any of this had ever happened.

He'd had enough of this girl for a lifetime.

Tomas was just about to close his eyes for the evening when he thought he saw the shadows move off in the distance. He kept his body still. "Elzeth?"

In response to his request, Tomas's vision sharpened. Vague shadows became stark outlines and the world grew brighter.

At first, Tomas saw nothing. The path was empty. Then he caught a hint of movement, a head ducking behind a rock. Now that he knew where to look, he watched and waited.

Beside him, Lyana drifted off to sleep, her breath coming slow and easy.

The head creeped around the corner again, raising itself like a crocodile floating with just its eyes above water.

It was a man, with neatly trimmed salt-and-pepper hair. Tomas watched, and the man did the same. After a few seconds, the unwelcome visitor squinted. Then he stood up. Tomas received his first full look at the man. The clothes he wore had once been white, were now stained with layers of dirt. Tomas couldn't miss the emblem on the man's breast, though. Three wavy lines, stitched with red thread.

As if this little side trip hadn't been hard enough.

The man smiled and bowed. Then he waved to Tomas and retreated into the forest.

Tomas considered pursuing him, but only for a moment. The girl was peacefully asleep and that was all he desired, too. Let the churchman try to sneak up on him. He'd pay for the mistake with his life.

"You good?" he asked Elzeth.

"I'm good."

"Thanks," Tomas said.

He closed his eyes and fell asleep, content to leave the mysteries of this mountain for another explorer.

14

Tomas woke the next morning, surprised to find himself well rested. Trouble had seemed almost a certainty last night. "Nothing?" he asked.

"Not even a squirrel," Elzeth replied.

Tomas yawned and scratched at an itch at the back of his neck. "Weird place."

"You always did have a gift for understatement." Elzeth's tone was glib, but Tomas could feel his unease.

Lyana looked like she hadn't moved a single muscle since the night before. Asleep, she looked smaller somehow. He feared that if he blinked she would disappear, swallowed up by the enormous vistas that surrounded them.

She was a lot of trouble for such a small girl.

One of these days, he'd learn to stop sticking his nose in problems that weren't his own.

The war was over. Fighting for anything beyond survival was a young man's cause, and he should know better. The world was too big and too cruel a place, and those kind-hearted souls who tried to save everyone eventually went mad with despair.

He would see the girl safe. He didn't like leaving anything unfinished. Now that he'd started, he might as well see it to its conclusion. The act wasn't much, and he had no belief that it somehow balanced out lives he'd taken, but it was something.

He searched through his pack while Lyana dozed. Hopefully, Tatum and his wife were as generous on his second visit as they had been on his first. The girl had eaten through nearly a week's worth of food in the short time he had known her, and he suspected she would be hungry again today.

She burned too fast.

He had a little food left. Enough for what amounted to one light day of eating. If the girl ate as much as he expected, it wouldn't last them past lunch.

Fortunately, he was used to traveling hungry. Lyana needed the energy, otherwise the sagani residing within her would begin devouring her from within. The emaciated hosts they'd fought off recently were examples of the process in action.

He pulled out a measured amount of food for breakfast and packed the rest. His pack was the lightest it had been in months.

Lyana woke while he ate, as though the sound of him chewing had summoned her from the land of sleep and dream. He held out her portion of food.

She took it and bowed her head in thanks, but Tomas saw the look on her face.

"Sorry, food is running out, and we only have enough to get back to the doctor's."

He caught her skeptical look at his pack.

After everything, he felt like he'd earned a bit of trust, but he couldn't blame her. Given what little he knew of her, he imagined trust didn't come easy. "You can check if you want. We've got what's in front of us and one meal for lunch. And I haven't yet seen anything on this mountain that I want to eat."

Thankfully, she didn't argue. But from the way she kept looking up the mountain instead of down, it was easy enough to guess her true desires.

He worried what would happen after he left her, then violently discarded the thought. Only so much could be asked of a man. He would get her to safety. What happened after that was none of his business.

They ate the rest of their breakfast quickly. Tomas had let the girl sleep. She needed her rest both for the long day of travel ahead and for the evolution gripping her body. But now that she was awake, his only desire was to put as much distance between him and the mountain as possible.

Lyana let him lead the way down. They entered the pine forest, and Tomas kept his eyes open for the mysterious man from the church. The more he thought about last night's encounter, the more it unsettled him. They'd been separated by a considerable distance, and there was no way the churchman should have known he was observed.

Perhaps the man had remarkable vision, or an uncanny sense of intuition, but neither of those explanations sat well with Tomas. On the other hand, the man hadn't displayed even a hint of madness, nor did he appear to suffer from the bizarre symptoms that afflicted so many hosts on this mountain.

Whatever Tomas' concerns, no further danger seemed forthcoming. There was no sign of the man. As they continued their descent, Tomas began to convince himself that he'd seen a ghost.

They made good time. The girl was a quiet companion,

but she kept his pace without complaint. Her first words to him came early in the afternoon. "I'm getting hungry," she said.

Tomas looked around. He'd made this ascent in the middle of the night, but he thought he had a pretty good idea of where he was. "I remember a little vantage point up ahead. Can you hold out another half mile or so?"

She grimaced but nodded.

Tomas' memory proved reliable, and before long they came upon a small outcropping of rock that allowed them to look over the foothills and into the land beyond. By the time they sat down, Tomas had to admit he was ready for lunch, too. He pulled out the last of his food, divided it, and then opened his pack to her to prove that it was empty. She rolled her eyes and they began their meal.

Lyana surprised him by speaking first. "How long have you been a host?"

"Too long," Tomas said. At her unsatisfied look he added, "Many years."

"Why haven't you gone mad yet?"

Tomas nibbled at his food. He supposed it wasn't a secret, exactly. He'd kept it private to protect himself. Becoming a host came with a cost most weren't willing to pay.

Which was a good thing.

Fewer hosts made the world a much safer place, both for him and for others.

But keeping it to himself doomed the girl to an early death.

"The more you use your abilities, the faster you'll go mad," he said. "Imagine that you have a cup of sand. Whenever you use your ability, you dump out a bit of that sand. The more you use, the more sand you dump."

"And when the cup is empty, I go mad?"

"Except worse. This isn't exact, mind you, but when the cup gets half empty, you'll start to develop your first tics. And the power will get harder to control, so you'll lose more, faster. And you'll get more tics and lose more control."

"Is that what happened to the other prospectors?"

"I think so. It's a little like slipping down the side of a mountain. If your foot slips just a little and you catch yourself, it's not a problem at all. But the farther you tumble, the faster you fall." Tomas paused to make sure she was paying attention. "And that's why this place is so dangerous to us. I can't say why, but it's extremely difficult to control our strength here. Even with years of practice, I almost lost control completely."

Lyana absorbed the news quietly. "So, I have all this strength, but I can't use it?"

"Not if you want to live a long and healthy life," Tomas said.

Lyana finished her meal. "I want to use it," she admitted. "It's like my body is demanding it."

"If you can control the desire for long enough, that will fade a bit. But it never goes away. And that's doubly true on this mountain. That's why we need to get you off it."

For the first time, it looked like he'd earned her agreement. She stood, eager to be off.

Out of the corner of his eye, Tomas caught the sight of movement. He glanced over and saw what appeared to be a spider. But it was too large.

A sagani.

The spider-like creature hurried away, but something about it made Tomas rub his arms, suddenly cold despite the midday sun.

15

Tomas finished his meal while Lyana tapped her foot, impatiently waiting.

Now, she seemed almost as eager to get off the mountain as him. As soon as he was done, she helped him pack.

Tomas led the way, and when he glanced back from time to time, he swore he caught her skipping behind him.

He reassured himself that she would be fine.

If his own childhood had taught him anything, it was that children were plenty resilient. If she had some support for the next few years, she would do well for herself. She was already smart and tough.

Some small part of him was even curious to see the woman she might become.

The forest grew thick around them, swallowing sounds and blocking the sun.

Tomas couldn't wait to leave these woods behind. After months of traveling the wide plains, he was used to silence, but this silence possessed an unsettling quality. Even in the open prairie, songbirds chirped their songs and coyotes howled at night. There was none of that here. He expected to hear the quick patter of squirrel feet as they scampered from tree to tree, or the mating call of one bird to another.

But the only sound he heard was their feet walking through a bed of dead pine needles. The silence was oppressive.

He caught sight of another one of the spider-shaped sagani. Or perhaps the same one from earlier. It paralleled them, keeping about a hundred feet to their left.

Tomas kept an eye on it, but didn't think much of it.

When a second joined the first, it caught his full attention.

When the third joined, his heart started to beat faster. The sagani kept pace with them, moving through the forest on silent limbs. Lyana saw them, too. Tomas walked faster, setting a more demanding pace. Lyana followed, her shorter legs churning to keep up.

A hundred feet to their left, the sagani increased their pace, too.

Tomas turned to Lyana. "Can you run?"

She nodded, her eyes wide and fixed on the sagani.

"Lyana."

She tore her gaze away from the predators and looked at him.

"We're going to run, and when you get tired, you're going to want to use your new strength. It will feel like the right choice. You need to fight it. Do you understand?"

She gave him one quick, sharp nod.

He believed she would try.

The only question was whether she had the will to over-come the trial she would soon face.

Tomas started with by jogging slowly. He glanced back to make sure Lyana was keeping pace, and then he ran.

The sagani skittered along quickly, their legs almost a blur.

The girl held him back. Alone, he would risk using Elzeth and return to safety within an hour or two. But the danger to her was too great, and he couldn't carry her that far.

So they ran, the sagani effortlessly keeping up. Fortunately, they seemed content to pace the pair. They never approached closer. Tomas hadn't come close to too many sagani in his life, but he'd never observed this type of behavior. Hadn't heard any stories like this, either.

He didn't care to understand.

Once he was off the mountain, it could keep its mysteries for an age.

Lyana uttered a small cry. When Tomas looked back, two more of the spider-shaped sagani had joined them, this time to their right. "Just keep running," he said.

Up ahead, the game trail they'd been following bifurcated. Tomas intended to take the trail to the left. It led down the mountain to the stream he'd followed up earlier.

A hulking shadow stepped onto the trail on the left. It stood on two legs, but its four arms marked it as a sagani. Tomas guessed it was eight feet tall and half again as heavy as he was. It looked like it had claws, too.

Tomas reconsidered his choices and took the trail to the right.

Almost immediately, the trail bent so they were no longer descending, but instead running across the mountain. The spiders that had been on their right slowed and then followed, maintaining the same spacing as before. The ones on the left disappeared as Tomas and Lyana turned, but reappeared less than a minute later.

Tomas slowed, then stopped running.

Behind him, Lyana was breathing hard. Tomas had little doubt she was used to long days on the road and endless miles of walking, but this was something different. Still, she hadn't succumbed to the desire to unleash her new abilities, which impressed him. "Why are we stopping?" she gasped.

"We're being herded," Tomas said.

He closed his eyes and tried to summon Elzeth's memories from the time before he'd become a host. "Do the sagani often cooperate like this?" he asked.

"I have no memory of doing so."

Tomas couldn't dredge one up, either. "Any ideas?"

"Break through and see how they react."

That had been Tomas' idea, too. He loved it when they agreed.

He turned left, down the slope. The woods were thick, but the underbrush wasn't impassable. "Follow me," he told Lyana.

He started down the slope, angling left. They should cross paths with the trail Tomas had intended to take, hopefully well behind where the tall sagani stood.

The trio of spider-like sagani moved to block his way. They'd turned from escorts into guards.

"Can you move them?" Tomas asked.

"I'll try," Elzeth replied. Elzeth shouted, the soundless roar vibrating Tomas' bones and making his stomach feel sick.

Tomas sensed them respond, but the language had no human equivalent. They didn't budge.

"I don't think they're going to let us pass," Elzeth said.

Tomas weighed his options, then reached for his sword. Elzeth didn't complain, which was as close to agreement as they were going to come.

"Help!"

Tomas swore and spun around. He'd forgotten Lyana for a moment, and he saw the two sagani that had been pacing them to the right were now less than a dozen paces away and closing fast.

"Stay close behind me," he said.

Tomas drew his sword and attacked the group of three spiders. They spread out as he approached, but they didn't retreat an inch. He angled left, choosing a direction at random, and the whole line shifted to keep him hemmed in.

No matter. He'd expected to have to cut through them anyway. He sliced, but the sagani he attacked was no longer there. Tomas glanced left and right, in time to see both of the other spiders approach. But he didn't know where the center one had gone.

The sagani moved faster than any human or spider, and when the first one hit him, he felt like someone had struck him in the side with a yard of heavy lumber. Tomas spun and cut, slicing nothing but empty air. One of the spiders landed on his back, almost bringing him to his knees.

Behind him, Lyana cried out again, and something fell heavily to the ground.

Maybe, if he was alone, he could have fought through.

He wasn't even tempted to leave her behind. He took a few steps back, and all five of the spider-like sagani arranged themselves in front of him. So long as he didn't take a step forward, they didn't seem very interested in him.

He risked a glance back. Lyana had been knocked over, but was getting shakily to her feet. "You hurt?" he asked.

She looked down at herself. "I don't think so."

He could hear her breaths as she struggled to control them.

She sounded close to giving in to the power within her.

"You're doing great," Tomas said, taking another step

back. The spiders didn't follow. He took her arm and guided her back to the path. Her breathing slowed, and Tomas' own heart beat slower.

They were still alive, so they had options.

But right now, it seemed like someone, or something, really didn't want them getting off the mountain.

16

Tomas eyed the sagani with all the hate he could muster, hoping that if he stared hard enough, they would catch on fire, explode, or disintegrate before him. Unfortunately, the sagani remained impervious to his stares. Two of the creatures had made a wide circle around them and were once again higher up on the mountain, ready to escort them onward. The other three were below, in a loose line that shifted whenever Tomas moved.

Beside him, Lyana was doubled over, hands on knees, fighting to control her breathing. When he tried to help, she gave him a glare so fierce he'd retreated three steps before he was consciously aware of the reaction.

He let her fight her battles alone, as she wished.

The girl had a spine of steel, equal to any of the selfless heroes he'd fought beside or against in the war.

Problem was, it was the heroes who went to the gate before their time. The girl deserved better. She had nothing but trials ahead of her, though.

"Any luck?" Tomas asked. His own stomach had been

twisting as Elzeth attempted to communicate with the sagani.

"It's like trying to talk to a wall," Elzeth said. "They aren't even reacting anymore."

"Don't suppose you've come up with an explanation that makes a lick of sense?"

Elzeth's silence was answer enough.

Tomas raised his arms above his head, stretched, and yawned. His muscles ached from the long days of use and limited rest. The sun had already fallen below the peaks of the mountains, and it wouldn't be long before the sky lost its color.

Tomas didn't think they'd make it to Tatum's tonight.

He didn't even have a plan for getting there tomorrow.

Lyana's breathing evened out again, and soon she straightened. "I'm good," she said. "But maybe we can walk for a bit?"

The girl looked twice as tired as Tomas felt, and he had to remind himself that for everything he'd been through the last few days, it was nothing compared to the challenges she had faced. The fact that she was alive, on her feet, and moving, spoke more to her character than anything she could say.

Tomas looked at the unmoving sagani. It didn't matter whether they crawled or ran. He nodded, and set a gentle pace following the trail.

The sagani escorted them.

Soon, they would have to rest for the night. Running had done nothing but bring Lyana to the brink of utter exhaustion. The temptation to use her new strength grew the weaker she became. If she had a mile left in her tonight, he'd be surprised.

He didn't think the sagani would bother them as they

slept. So long as they didn't proceed any farther down the mountain, the sagani seemed perfectly harmless.

Which by itself was unusual. It was hard to generalize when it came to sagani, but they weren't terribly peaceful most days. They were the only predators that made a human think twice about leaving the safety of their town.

"Tomas." Elzeth's warning was quiet but urgent.

His gaze shot up, and he realized he'd been lost in thought. He looked to the left and right, but the sagani weren't there. Hope sprang to life in his chest, and he turned quickly around to share it with Lyana.

His budding hope died when he understood what happened. Nearly a hundred feet behind him, Lyana had fallen to her hands and knees.

The girl was closer to giving in than Tomas had realized. Her toughness deceived him. They needed to rest, and much sooner rather than later.

It wasn't Lyana, though, that killed his hopes of escaping the mountain. It was the sagani.

They'd closed in on Lyana, and all five were barely a dozen feet from her. Tomas ran toward them, closing the distance quickly. As he neared, the sagani backed off to their customary distance.

Tomas stopped a few paces short of Lyana. She hated his assistance, which left him unsure of how to help her. Lacking any more useful action, he stood guard over her as she fought the temptations raging within.

A few minutes later, she moved into a comfortable sitting position. When she looked at him, the fire in her stare had almost flickered out. Her eyes pleaded with him, but she wouldn't admit the weakness out loud.

"Will you let me carry you?" he asked. "We'll find a place to camp."

She nodded, and Tomas picked her up in his arms. She was too light, and he had no more food to offer. Was she already slipping away?

He carried her another quarter mile along the trail until he found a suitable place to make camp. Once she was comfortable, he told her he was going to search for any food. She gave him a weak wave that he took for acknowledgment. She didn't look like she believed in his success any more than he did.

Tomas left the camp, but he kept looking back, unwilling to let the girl out of his sight.

As he feared, the farther away he walked, the closer their sagani escort came to the girl. By the time he was a hundred feet away, they'd circled the camp tightly.

None of the sagani followed him.

Tomas studied the scene and swore softly. He rubbed the exhaustion from his eyes.

The trail leading down the mountain was empty.

"Tell me we aren't thinking this," Tomas said.

"I am," Elzeth admitted quietly.

Tomas continued to watch. The sagani seemed content to surround the girl for the moment. He doubted they'd be so harmless if he surrendered to his own temptation. She'd be gone before he'd walked a mile down the hill.

"She's just one life in a vast wilderness," Elzeth said. His words were empty, a cup shaped by reason but without a drop of heart. But they needed to be said. Needed to be considered.

Tomas didn't move.

"We could go back to Tatum's and come back with more food, better prepared to help her."

They both knew the likely outcome of that choice. That was nothing more than a lie they would tell themselves to feel better. Once they were down, Tomas wasn't sure he'd return. Once the first justification was accepted, the others followed rapidly behind.

Tomas swore again.

He'd just as soon be on the walls of a fortress besieged by a much more powerful army.

"The odds the girl survives, no matter what we do, are low," Elzeth said.

The corner of Tomas' mouth turned up in a bitter smile. "That's enough. Thanks."

Elzeth bowed and stopped arguing.

Tomas watched for a moment longer, making peace with his choice.

He walked toward the girl, and as he did, the spider-like sagani broke away and returned to their posts away from the camp. Tomas didn't think they would try anything while he was near. And if they did, Elzeth would warn him.

"I'm tired of saying the words," Tomas admitted.

He felt the soft glow of satisfaction from the center of his stomach.

"Me too," Elzeth said.

17

Tomas woke to Elzeth's warning shout. He was standing, sword in hand, before he even knew why he'd been alerted.

It didn't take him long to figure out. The spider-like sagani skittered toward Lyana, faster than any creature had a right to move. Elzeth blazed to life.

The transition came easier than before, but it still took Tomas several precious seconds to have full control over his body. Before he could move, the sagani were on top of Lyana. She woke instantly, shouting as the creatures crawled over her. Two reached for her legs, their front limbs terminating with hooked appendages.

The hooks dug into Lyana's legs. She screamed louder and tried to kick them off, but the sagani's grip was stronger. They pulled Lyana up the mountain as though dragging a sack of potatoes. She clawed the ground for anything to hold onto, but her desperate hands found nothing.

One of the sagani followed the two with Lyana, while the last two stood guard between Tomas and the girl.

As soon as he was sure he was in control of his body,

Tomas leaped forward. One of the sagani skittered forward and jumped to meet him. It hurtled through the air like a bullet shot from an oversized rifle.

This time, though, it didn't matter. Tomas had Elzeth's aid, and his sword was already drawn and ready. He cut, and his sword was just in time. The blade sliced the sagani in two, and it died wordlessly.

The last of the guard sagani shifted left and right, moving too fast to offer Tomas a clean strike.

Tomas ignored the distraction. He angled toward Lyana, already ten feet away from camp. Her upper body twisted and fought like a crazed animal, but the spiders' grip on her legs was unyielding.

When the guard sagani realized Tomas was about to pass by, it changed tactics. It skittered backward at an angle, again posting itself between Tomas and the kidnapping.

Tomas was ready, hoping for the change in position. One predictable move was all he needed.

He cut, and for once, the sagani was right where he expected it. The second guard joined the first in whatever waited the creatures after death.

Tomas' stomach cramped, Elzeth groaning as a thick darkness threatened to smother Elzeth's flame. The assault only lasted a moment, and Elzeth burned through it. Tomas didn't have time to wonder what had just happened.

Above them, Lyana's struggles ceased so suddenly Tomas worried she had died. Her body went limp. Immediately, the two sagani pulling her released their grip. They joined the sagani who'd so far remained separate from the battle, and together the three advanced on Tomas.

The fact he'd killed two sagani tonight was remarkable enough. They were tough creatures, and strong and fast to boot. But their attacks had been clumsy. And though giant spiders might possess some advantages as a shape, they weren't nearly as dangerous as some of the forms Tomas had seen them take.

These weren't the sagani he was used to.

Still, he didn't think that would save him from three attacking him at once. Especially if they had any level of coordination.

"It's not too late to run," Elzeth said.

Tomas grunted.

The sagani in the middle raced toward him, its hooked appendages slicing at his legs. Tomas stabbed at it, but missed as it shifted to the side. He was forced to retreat to protect his calves.

The second sagani that had been pulling Lyana disappeared into a clump of bushes, appearing again a few moments later to Tomas' right. Tomas twisted in an attempt to keep both sagani in view.

Fortunately, the third sagani still didn't seem interested in fighting. It moved closer, but just to put itself in a better position to observe.

Behind the supervising sagani, Lyana suddenly sat up straight, her back as stiff as a board. She tilted her head, as though listening to a voice calling for her from far away.

"That can't be good," Elzeth muttered.

Tomas' head twisted back and forth, trying to keep both sagani in view. They attacked from opposite directions. He stepped toward the one on his right, hoping to disrupt whatever coordination they possessed.

It only caused the one on the left to leap at him.

He danced nimbly away from the first attack, but both sagani advanced relentlessly. He batted aside one just as the other hooked into his calf. Tomas roared and stabbed down, but the sagani tore its hook out as it leaped backward. He twisted on his good leg, barely avoiding another hook.

One of the sagani leaped for his chest, catching him in a position where he had no good response. Its hooks dug deep into his pectorals.

The sagani was too close to bring his sword to bear, so Tomas took the first action that came to mind. He smashed his forehead against the sagani's body.

Tomas cursed as stars exploded in his vision. The thing felt like a brick. He swore he heard the sagani laughing at him, though they rarely made any sound.

The blow at least knocked some sense into him. He reached for the knife at his hip, fingers grasping for the hilt. The sagani tore deeper into his flesh, scrambling over him like it was already looking for the tastiest morsel of his corpse to eat.

Before he reached his knife, the sagani suddenly went limp. The hooks released their grip as the sagani fell to the ground. Lyana stood before him, sword in hand.

He hadn't even made sense of the scene before she went after the final aggressive sagani. Injured, and without using him as bait, she had no chance. Fast as she was, the sagani was faster.

But they had turned the tables on the sagani. It was two of them against one, and the last sagani still appeared to have no interest in doing anything but watching.

Finally, both surviving sagani skittered away. Lyana followed for a dozen paces, then stopped when she saw Tomas wasn't following. Just as suddenly as Tomas had woken up, the woods were quiet once again.

He cleaned his sword and sheathed it, then walked over to Lyana. He could almost feel the heat radiating off her. She was in control, though. On this mountain, that was no small feat.

Before he reached her, her eyes rolled up in her head and she collapsed to the ground. Tomas caught her as she fell. For the second time that night, he carried her to the camp. With Elzeth's help, it was easy, even with his injuries.

Once she seemed comfortable, he let go of Elzeth.

They'd both been far too active lately.

He watched their surroundings for a while, but the forest was as quiet as ever. Eventually, his eyes started to feel heavy. It had been one hell of a day.

"Can you take watch again?" he asked.

"Sure," Elzeth said. "Get some rest."

Tomas didn't need to be told twice.

18

Tomas woke, yawned, and stretched, embracing the last few minutes of relaxation he was going to get this day. The sagani had left them alone for the rest of the night, and he'd slept like a rock. For a few precious moments, all was right with the world.

It didn't take long for the reality of their situation to cast a long shadow over his disposition, though.

He sat up and rubbed his eyes. The sun was higher than he expected, but the forest that surrounded him remained stubbornly silent. If not for the breeze brushing the tops of the pines, there would have been no sound at all.

Lyana slept, dead to the world.

Tomas let her rest. He stood up and took stock of their situation.

The sight made him jump. He bit off his shout before it left his lips. Better to let Lyana rest undisturbed.

Elzeth chuckled. "Thought you would like that."

The corpses of the sagani they had killed last night were gone, but they'd been replaced by even more of the creatures. Tomas guessed there were at least ten scattered in a loose circle around the camp. "I'm not sure I've ever seen so many in one place. And certainly never so many take the same form."

"It's making me think I'm missing out on something important," Elzeth said. "But I wasn't talking about the sagani."

Tomas looked around again. A small pack lay on a rock about thirty feet west of their camp. He grunted.

"One of them brought it down this morning, a little before dawn. Dragged it from higher up and left it there."

"And you didn't wake me?"

"Almost did. But it wasn't getting any closer, and you needed rest."

Tomas looked at the pack. "Any idea what's inside?"

"Not the slightest."

Tomas approached warily. He drew his sword and lifted the top flap. The scents that wafted out from the bag made his mouth water. He poked around with his sword a bit, just to make sure there were no surprises. Then he sheathed the blade.

It was food, and a fair quantity. Enough for both of them for two, maybe three days. He pulled out a strip of dried meat and ate it. He felt no ill effects, so he grabbed the pack and brought it back to where Lyana slept.

Most of her wounds from the night before had already healed. He chalked it up to her age, but it worried him a bit. She was pushing too hard, even at rest. He had no true idea how far one had to push before the tics started setting in. But he'd seen relatively new hosts with a range of tics, and had always erred on the side of caution.

Lyana didn't wake for another hour.

When she did, she displayed no obvious tics. That, at least, was one worry he could ignore for the day. He offered her food, which she eyed suspiciously. "Where did you get this?"

He tilted his head toward the sagani. "They brought it."

She looked at the collection of creatures, then back at him. "That doesn't make a lick of sense."

"No, it does not." Tomas took another bite.

Lyana didn't look convinced, but the demands of her body overwhelmed any last shreds of resistance.

"Why are you still here?" she asked between bites. "They would have left you alone."

It was a good question. One he wished he had a better answer to. "Didn't seem right."

"Noble, but misguided." She took another bite. "You know what's happening, don't you? You know the mountain wants me."

Tomas nodded. He held up the meat in his hand. "Alive, too. At least for now."

"There's nothing you can do to save me." She noticed his reaction. "You know that, too. So why not save yourself?"

She was right. It seemed her fate had been sealed the moment she started climbing this mountain. And yet, here he was, raging against the inevitable.

"Couldn't say." He frowned as a nagging question surfaced in his thoughts. "Why west?"

She gave him a confused look.

"When your father was attacked, you were bathing, right? That's how you hid from them?"

"Yes. They weren't looking terribly hard for survivors."

"Why go west? Why not run back down the mountain to the doctor's house?"

Her answer came quickly. "Justice."

"Justice?"

Lyana stared down at her feet. "My father was a good

man with a streak of luck as rotten as a year-old cabbage. He could mine a vein so fast you wouldn't believe it possible. Life treated him poorly, though. Mom left him for another man, a banker the next town over. She'd never wanted kids or a family, but Pa had promised her gold when they were young. She left when it didn't come."

Lyana swallowed the lump in her throat. "He tried hard, raising me and finding ways to put food on the table, but no matter how hard he worked, he couldn't get ahead. When he heard the rumors of the untapped veins in these parts, he felt like he had to try. He offered to let me stay with his parents, but I wanted to be with him. It was a hell of a journey, but we made it here. Then he gets killed with his destination in sight."

She kept her face down, but Tomas saw no tears fall. "There was no justice in his life, but I intend for him to have it in death."

When she looked up, the fire in her eyes was blazing.

"The man who killed your father is dead," Tomas said.

"The body that killed my father is dead. But I don't believe for a moment that the true killer has been brought to justice. Do you?"

He was forced to admit he didn't.

Lyana finished her food. "I appreciate all you've done. Truly. But it's time for you to leave."

Tomas watched her as she began to pack her meager belongings. She gestured at the pack of food, and he nodded. She slung it over her shoulders. "You mean to see this through, don't you?" he asked.

"It wants me. Whatever it is. I don't know why or how, but it's going to let me close. And when it does, I plan on killing it, even if it's the last thing I do. Better a quick death than the fate of the men we've met thus far."

Tomas stood, too. He'd made his decision last night, so there wasn't much more deliberation required. "I'm not good at much, but I am good at killing. Might as well lend you a hand."

Lyana stared at him as though he were the one who had gone mad. He supposed the look wasn't entirely undeserved. "You'll die for no reason."

He met her gaze. "If I die, it'll be because I chose to help you. Good a reason as any, and a sight better than many."

"I mean your death won't do any good. Odds are, I'll fail. Dense as you are, even you must have figured that out by now. This is a trip that only goes one way, and it's a lost cause."

Tomas scratched the side of his face. He was starting to grow pretty decent stubble. When he got the chance, a shave would do him good.

"I was a soldier, back in the day," he said. "Fought in the war. Learned a lesson." He really did need to shave. Soon he would look like the hosts wandering this mountain. "We can't predict the future. It sounds obvious, but most people haven't quite figured it out. Knew plenty of kids who woke up on the eve of battle feeling invincible, and I suspect you're smart enough to guess how that went for 'em. I've seen certain victories slip through grasping fingers, and I've been sure I was dead at least half a dozen times, yet here I stand. You're right enough when you say the odds don't look good, but nothing's impossible."

Lyana studied him, silent as she considered his statement.

"I didn't know you were capable of stringing so many words together," Elzeth said.

The comment made him smile. However the girl felt about it, Elzeth agreed with the decision. For Tomas, that was what mattered. Let the world think what it would. The only opinion worth anything was the one that shared his thoughts.

Finally, Lyana shrugged. "Fine. You want to die, you can come with. But you better not slow me down."

Tomas gave her a short bow. "Wouldn't dream of it."

19

L yana barely waited for him to finish packing before leaving. Her gait was different now. She moved quickly and quietly, radiating confidence with every step. At times, she reminded him of a large cat prowling through the woods for prey.

He doubted she'd possessed such predatory instincts before.

Her evolution neared its conclusion, right before his eyes. A host was always more than the human it had once been, the sum of a mysterious equation no academic could solve.

Tomas hadn't fought beside another host since the war. He found, to his surprise, that he missed it. Most humans couldn't understand what it meant to share both body and thoughts with another creature.

Lyana did.

Her strides were longer than the ones he'd followed up the mountain several days ago. Her eyes swept left and right, and she paused frequently to listen. Though untrained, she had become one of the most dangerous people on the mountain. Tomas wondered if she was equal to the task she'd set for herself. He'd doubted earlier. Now, it seemed a tantalizing possibility.

It took him nearly an hour to realize he'd forgotten to ask an obvious question. "Do you know where you're going?"

She pointed up the mountain. "The camp we saw in our visions is over there," she said.

Half a dozen questions popped into his head, but there was no real point in asking them. She wouldn't know the answers. Instinct and intuition guided her, bubbling up from a mysterious source. The sagani escorted the pair, and the creatures did nothing to impede their progress.

Lyana was meant to go up there.

And Tomas, fool that he was, followed.

The forest thickened, dimming the sky as they followed the narrow trail. The earthy scent of pine was even stronger here, overwhelming all other smells. At times, Tomas saw evidence of other humans. Theirs weren't the first boots to follow this trail.

When the path split in two, Lyana chose without hesitation. They now traveled south and west, slowly gaining elevation as they picked their way around the mountain.

Lyana stopped so suddenly Tomas almost ran into her. She stared through the trees, then bobbed her head as though she'd seen exactly what she expected. Tomas followed her gaze but saw nothing. He felt the heat radiating off her skin.

He almost warned her from continuing to use her powers, but held his tongue. Though young, she knew the consequences, and was old enough to choose this much. She didn't believe she would live long.

"We're almost there," she said, pointing to a gap in the trees that revealed nothing to Tomas' eyes. "Any ideas?"

"The more we know, the better," Tomas said. "If we can get closer without being seen, we might learn something useful."

Lyana looked to their sagani escorts, waiting in perfect stillness to each side. "I'm not sure we can approach unseen."

Warmth rose in his cheeks. He'd gotten too used to their companions. "No harm in trying."

She smiled, an expression that told him she understood his mistake and was willing to let him save some small amount of face.

They moved from tree to tree, Lyana still in the lead. Slowly, the sight before them revealed itself to Tomas' unaided eyes.

His sense of remembrance was overpowering. The clearing was exactly as he'd seen it in the flash of his vision. Yet it was a memory he'd never experienced in person.

They looked into a wide clearing, one partly created by human hands. It was almost a perfect circle, with a steep rise forming the western boundary. Stumps of pine ran along the edge of the clearing, but Tomas couldn't see what the lumber was being used for.

A handful of tents were scattered throughout the clearing, erected in no particular order Tomas could discern. Most looked to have been sloppily constructed, as though they'd been set up by drunks and no one had ever bothered to fix them. A well-worn trail on the western edge of the clearing led up the steep rise, quickly disappearing higher up the mountain.

Supplies looked like they'd been thrown around in a fit

of madness. Tomas spotted saws, a few axes, and several pots and pans. Strangely, he saw no evidence of a cookfire.

No one moved among the tents, and he stepped forward to enter the clearing for a closer look. Lyana held out her hand, freezing him in place.

Moments later, two men appeared on the trail above the camp. They stumbled down the path, reinforcing Tomas' belief the whole camp was constantly inebriated. It would explain the sloppiness of their home.

Then he saw the shudders that ran through their bodies, clear as day.

He swallowed the lump in his throat. It should be impossible. By now, he shouldn't be surprised, and yet, he was. Hosts were uncommon. And yet this mountain was teeming with them. Far too many to be of natural causes.

He thought of the host pushing Lyana off the ledge, and the sagani that had been so close.

It all seemed far more intentional now.

The hosts reached the clearing and walked straight to where a set of axes lay. Each man picked one up and proceeded to a pine at the edge of the clearing. They went to work with powerful swings, far stronger than human hands could achieve on their own.

Chunks of tree spun in all directions as the men chopped. The hosts didn't so much as blink, even as slivers of wood bounced off their cheeks and foreheads.

The tree fell before long, almost crushing one of the men who failed to step clear quickly enough. Once down, the men went to work again, cutting off entire limbs of the tree with single swings.

Those men were nearly as dangerous with their axes as he was with his sword.

Just as the men finished, others came down the mountain. Eight total. Together, they began hauling the log up the mountain trail. They were led by an older man, hair white and long.

The whole scene disturbed Tomas. Start to finish, the task had lasted less than an hour, but none of the men had uttered a single word to one another. He watched them leave, now curious where the trail led, and to what purpose the logs were being used.

He wasn't curious enough to break cover, though.

"So, now what do you think?" Lyana asked him.

"I haven't the slightest clue," Tomas admitted, "but I suspect you're going to tell me that you're going to head up that trail."

"It's in the mountain," she said. "It always has been."

Before Tomas could answer, the men hauling the log were greeted by another man, who now stood in the spot right before the trail turned and disappeared.

Tomas had seen the man before, but never in the light of day. The symbol over his breast practically glowed. The churchman looked to exactly where they were, smiled, and waved.

Then he followed the others, disappearing higher up the mountain.

As soon as they disappeared, the now-familiar sound of skittering legs could be heard behind them. Tomas turned to see a group of the sagani cutting off their retreat.

He was starting to feel an awful lot like a marionette having his strings pulled.

20

"So much for hiding," Lyana smirked.

Tomas stepped away from the tree he'd been hiding behind and stretched. Behind him, even more of the spider-like sagani gathered. They formed a line that bent around the pair, preventing travel in any direction but forward.

Out of curiosity, Tomas approached the line.

The sagani gathered closer, cutting off his departure. Sharp hooks waved threateningly at him. They didn't speak, but their intent was more than clear.

Tomas grunted, then returned to Lyana. She stared at the place where the churchman had vanished. He didn't need to be psychic to guess her desire. He glanced back at the sagani. The girl would get her wish soon enough.

Lyana led the way into the clearing. Before she could start following the trail up the mountain, Tomas caught her attention. "Let's search the camp. There might be answers. Or food."

It wasn't until he mentioned food that she appeared

interested. But she agreed, and together they explored the odd camp.

Tomas lifted the flap on one tent to reveal a disorganized mess. Clothes were scattered all about and an empty pack lay in the corner. It smelled of rot. He let the flap drop and walked to another tent. This one had been constructed so poorly a strong breeze might knock it over. When he peeked in, though, the inside was nearly spotless. A full pack rested along one side of the tent, the buckles still closed. The bedroll hadn't even been laid out.

Tomas got down onto hands and knees and crawled in. He unbuckled the pack and looked through the contents. He found clothes and cooking supplies, followed by an assortment of trail necessities. None appeared to have been touched recently. And no food, unfortunately.

He exited the tent just as Lyana emerged from another tent. "Find anything interesting?" he asked.

"Nothing that makes sense. The tents are either really messy or really clean, though."

Tomas lifted the tent flaps of the tents Lyana had checked. She spoke true. More tents were clean than messy. Not because the habitants were tidy, but because the tents looked like they were barely used.

A pattern tickled the edges of his awareness. He stood in the center of tents, trying to bring the system to light.

Lyana tapped her foot, her gaze constantly returning to the mountains.

Tomas ignored her. He looked at each tent from his position, and then he had it.

The tents that looked like they were about to fall over were clean. The ones erected well were filled with the contents of whatever the prospectors had carried up.

But what did that tell him?

He didn't know, but it unsettled him.

There was a rustling from beyond the edge of the clearing. From the south.

More of the spider sagani appeared, but this time they were dragging a deer carcass. The poor animal hadn't died well. Tomas noted the punctures and deep cuts.

The sagani pulled the deer a dozen feet into the clearing, then released their hooks and returned to the woods. Tomas stared, dumbfounded.

"Did they just bring food?" Lyana asked.

"Seems that way."

Tomas looked again for evidence of a cookfire but found none. Had the hosts been eating the meat raw? He remembered the blood around the lips of some of the men.

If so, that wasn't the hosts' madness. At least not as Tomas understood it. He'd never seen or heard of such a thing.

The sagani that had been following them came into the clearing. They formed a line between Tomas, Lyana, and the deer. "Doesn't look they want to give us the time to prepare that meal," Lyana remarked.

He looked over at her. She had that smirk on her face again, as though the sagani's behavior was a justification of her own desires. "Doesn't it bother you that you're so eager to do exactly what they want?"

She patted the sword at her hip. "No. Our desires only line up to a point."

She certainly didn't lack confidence. Real or an act, he was impressed.

There was no point in delaying. The girl was right about one thing — their trail only led one direction.

"Then lead on," Tomas said. He only allowed himself a few seconds to stare longingly at the trail they'd come up, now crowded with sagani. He swore there were even more than before, as though Lyana was leading not just him, but all of them, to whatever awaited higher up the mountain.

"The next time you tell me to leave, remind me to listen," Tomas said to Elzeth.

"You think I'll ever let you forget this?" Elzeth replied. "Once we get off this mountain, I'm putting myself in charge of making all decisions."

"Probably for the best."

The trail leading from the camp turned out to be steeper than it looked. Tomas focused on putting one foot in front of the other. The backs of his legs burned as they gained elevation rapidly. They reached the turn where the men had vanished from sight.

Tomas spared one last look down. The sagani that had been following them clustered around the base of the trail, but they didn't follow any higher. He couldn't go down, but this was also the farthest he'd been from them in a day. It wasn't freeing, exactly, but there was a sense of possibility. That maybe there was still a way out of this.

Lyana didn't care. Her shorter legs continued to churn, her gaze focused on the mountains above.

Tomas hurried to catch up.

Less than a quarter mile up the path, Tomas caught the first look of their destination. The trail led up a valley to a dark hole. He swore under his breath and his step faltered. "Of course it would be a cave."

Elzeth chuckled.

Lyana kept her demanding pace, leaving him little time for his anxiety to bloom into panic. He caught up to her again and walked by her side. "You shouldn't go in there," he said.

She didn't even slow down. "It's in there."

"It's too dangerous."

She laughed. "Not any more than anything else on this mountain." She glanced at him, and his face told the story. "You don't have to come, if you're scared."

Tomas imagined walking into that cave, feeling the enormous weight of rock above him, ready to collapse at any moment. His palms were sweating, and he wiped them off on his pants. Half a dozen arguments came to his lips, but they all sounded weak, even to him.

Fighting every single one of the sagani waiting for him below seemed a much safer choice.

Lyana's pace made it clear she felt none of his hesitation.

They reached the cave. Here, it was plenty wide, but it quickly grew darker and more narrow.

"You won't be able to see a thing if you go in there," Tomas said.

Lyana pointed to a pile of torches in the corner. "I don't think we're the first ones to explore this particular cave. Can you start one for me?"

He almost refused, but then cursed his own cowardice. The girl was going in, one way or another. He lit two torches and handed her one.

She disappeared into the cave without so much as a glance back.

Tomas swallowed the lump in his throat and followed.

21

The cave narrowed, and Tomas imagined the walls pressing in on him as they picked their way down the steep decline. His breath came a little quicker at the thought.

In reality, the tunnel they descended was plenty spacious. Tomas stood without fear of hitting his head, and the walls were far enough apart they could walk two abreast with room to spare.

The tunnel narrowed slightly and they came upon a small chamber. Lyana held her torch aloft, no more bothered by being underground than standing in the middle of a wide-open field. "Where are all the men, and why did they carry the log up here?"

The question was legitimate, but Tomas found himself more concerned with how much rock was above them. Somewhere he couldn't see, water dripped onto the floor at an uneven cadence, echoing in the tunnel and in his thoughts.

"Don't suppose you could calm down?" Elzeth asked. "It's making control that much more difficult."

Tomas apologized. He tried to focus on his breath, the way he'd been taught since he was a child.

His techniques failed him. It felt like he wasn't getting enough air into his lungs, no matter how fast he breathed. He supported his weight against a wall and closed his eyes. But he couldn't focus. He was underground. The cold, damp air reminded him of the fact with every breath.

"You don't look so good," Lyana said. He felt the warm air as she brought her torch closer to him. When he closed his eyes, he could almost believe that it was the feel of the sun on his face.

"I don't like being underground."

"I'll not think less of you if you turn around," she said.

"Don't much care what you think of me."

She reached out and took his hand. "You've already risked your life. You have nothing to prove and nothing to gain."

Few temptations were stronger than the one to surrender. When pushing forward cost the most, it was the easiest thing in the world to just stop. By the hells, he'd given into the temptation in the past. He'd abandoned friends on the battlefield, convinced there was no way to save them. He'd given up on a woman he loved, once, because the challenges seemed impossible to overcome.

In hindsight, the decisions he'd made still seemed like the right ones.

But the heart had its own wisdom.

Surrender was easy.

But it led only to regret.

Lyana would not be another link in the chain of regrets he'd dragged across the frontier.

He was little good to her as he was, though. He shook his head. "Just give me a minute."

He handed her his torch, then found a place where he could sit cross-legged on the floor. He closed his eyes again.

Life only moved in one direction. He'd chosen to come with Lyana. She would never say so, but she wouldn't succeed if he didn't help. And death was death, whether it came at the sharp end of a blade or trapped underneath a mountain of rock.

The old words came to mind, the ones he had said over so many dead and dying.

His breathing slowed.

Elzeth calmed.

The fear remained. He didn't think he would live to see a day where he was comfortable in caves. But his defenses held. He opened his eyes and stood up. Lyana handed him the torch, curious about him but trying not to show it. "Lead the way," he said.

Lyana took them deeper into the mountain, and it wasn't long before they discovered where the wood had gone. The tunnel, once filled with jagged edges and uneven steps, smoothed out and widened.

No longer did they explore a work of nature.

Thick pieces of lumber supported the expansion, all of them relatively fresh. A few moments later, the sound of men at work reached their ears.

Tomas couldn't say if the men were around the corner or a half mile away. At times, the sound was so loud he was certain he was in the midst of the construction. Other times, it faded completely.

The only lights they saw were their own, though.

Lyana advanced cautiously, peering around every bend before proceeding.

They came upon the men.

The tunnel widened into a large chamber, and within

the chamber, most of the men were working. The sound of axes and saws was deafening. Only one torch lit the entire space, casting wicked shadows in all directions. They were preparing the wood for its place, likely farther into the tunnel.

Lyana observed them for a moment, then stepped into view before Tomas could stop her. He cursed and drew his sword. He didn't think he could fight against that many hosts in the best of circumstances. To fight so many in such a tight space was impossible. They would overwhelm him before he could cut them down.

Still, better a sword than suffocating to death, trapped in a place that had never seen sunlight.

Tomas looked for the man with the sign of the church on his breast, but he was nowhere to be found. Either he had gone deeper into the mountain or taken a path Tomas hadn't seen.

The men made no move toward Lyana. Their stares were blank, but one by one, they stopped their work to turn and look.

"I don't think they'll hurt us," she said. "It wants us here."

The men didn't react to her voice.

"I'd just as soon not test your theory," Tomas said, knowing full well the girl would continue to leave him with no choice.

To her credit, it looked like even she doubted the wisdom of stepping in the center of a collection of hosts. But fear slipped off the girl like hot oil in a pan. Maybe she wished for death. He didn't think she was ignorant of the risks.

Or maybe her desire to see her father avenged was that strong.

He couldn't begin to guess.

She took one step into the larger room, and then one more. The men cringed, as though they were staring at the sun. Then, one by one, they took a knee. They bowed their heads.

Tomas' insides twisted into a knot so tight he feared he would never stand straight again. He knew and understood the fear of death, but this fear was worse. It was a creeping dread, without reason or explanation.

"Elzeth?"

When the sagani replied, it felt like the equivalent of speaking through gritted teeth. "Whatever is here is strong. Too strong. Please," he paused, gathering his strength, "don't ask anything of me. Not here."

If the hosts around Lyana changed their attitudes, he wasn't sure what else he could do. But he would try to uphold the sagani's request.

Then another man appeared, emerging from the darkness of the tunnel on the other side of the room. He smiled, baring all his teeth, more hyena than man. He was the white-haired older man Tomas had seen earlier.

Like the others, he was a host.

But unlike the others, there was still a shred of intelligence in his gaze.

He twisted his head this way and that, and his jaw opened and closed, but no words came out. Something in his neck cracked, so loud it echoed in the small space.

His jaw moved again, and this time, words eventually emerged. They were dry and raspy, almost inhuman.

"Welcome."

22

The grizzled old man beckoned for them to follow him. He shuffled deeper into the tunnels, and Lyana followed. The prospectors held their bows as she passed. They stood as Tomas walked among them, their blank eyes glaring at him. Tomas' fingers itched to raise his sword and take heads.

In front of him, Lyana drew her own sword, holding it up like it was a torch.

This place went against all the laws of nature.

Tomas noted the walls of the tunnel. They'd been carved out by hand and reinforced by the pine trees from the camp below.

He knew little about mining. The only holes in the ground he had any familiarity with were graves, and he knew it took a group of men a decent bit of time to dig one of those. Tunneling into a mountain had to be several orders of magnitude more difficult. And there weren't that many men behind them. How long had they been here?

He almost asked, but he got the sense their host wasn't much for words.

The tunnel bent and then descended sharply. Stairs had been hewn into the stone, and they stepped down carefully. They came to a hole with a ladder.

The old man ignored the ladder and dropped into the hole. Tomas heard him land a moment later. He and Lyana poked their torches above the hole. The man looked up at them, standing on level ground. He beckoned for them to descend.

"You should let me go first," Tomas said.

Lyana ignored him and jumped down the hole.

Tomas shook his head. Children these days had no respect. Nor any wisdom.

He sheathed his sword, turned, and took the ladder. Even without Elzeth, the drop probably wouldn't hurt him, but why take any chances?

Once on the level below, he held the torch above his head and looked around. This new tunnel was quite a bit different than the ones above. There was nothing natural about it. The walls were smooth.

Too smooth, in fact. Tomas ran his hand along one of them and didn't feel so much as a bump. He couldn't think of a tool that made such smooth walls.

The head prospector, as Tomas was thinking of him, and Lyana were already twenty paces ahead by the time he followed them.

As he caught up, Tomas' stomach began to rumble. At first, he thought it was hunger.

But that made no sense. He'd eaten a good breakfast, and they hadn't been down in the tunnels that long.

"It doesn't want me here," Elzeth said.

"Then why hasn't it tried to stop us?"

"I'm getting the sense it isn't completely rational," Elzeth replied. "It's curious about us, but it considers us a threat. It can't decide if it wants us close or dead."

"Comforting."

Elzeth was silent for a while, then said, "It feels like a child. All emotion, tempered by only the slightest bit of reason."

"Don't suppose you have any explanations?"

Elzeth laughed bitterly.

Lyana stumbled as they neared an intersection. She leaned against a wall, then slid down it until she was sitting on the floor. Tomas came and squatted next to her. Their guide waited, impassive.

Sweat beaded down Lyana's brow, leaving streaks in the grime that covered her face. She grimaced. "Is it always like this?"

Tomas offered her his water skin, which she took gratefully. "There's nothing about this that's normal. Tell me what you're feeling."

She closed her eyes and leaned her head back against the wall. "There are three voices in my head. One is mine, the one I've always had. Then there's this one," she pointed to her stomach. "I don't hear her saying words, but I know what she's saying. Does that make any sense?"

Tomas nodded.

"But there's another one, the one I hear loudest of all. It's down there," she gestured down the tunnel, "and it wants me." She clutched at her stomach. "All the voices are arguing, and it feels like they're tearing my body apart."

Tomas wished he had something useful to say. The only answer he had was to leave the mountain as quickly as possible, but that wasn't happening anytime soon. "How can I help?"

"You're not going to give me your sword if I drop this one, are you? Yours seems sharper."

Tomas grinned and shook his head.

"Then just do me one favor." She winced. "If I'm ever not myself, I want you to kill me."

He opened his mouth to protest, but her glare silenced him.

"I mean it. I won't become a tool, like the men we've met. I'll live or die on my own terms." She stared into his eyes "Promise me."

He was the one who broke away from her stare first. "I'm not sure I can make that promise."

"Then what good are you?"

She used the wall to help her back to her feet. Her balance was off, but when Tomas offered a hand, she waved him away. She followed the host, ignoring Tomas as though he wasn't even there.

Tomas watched for a moment, his indecision taking on a new shape.

Perhaps he was a fool, but some part of him had always hoped there would be some sort of victory for Lyana.

He didn't believe that anymore.

The girl was set on a single path. Even if she somehow killed whatever lurked at the heart of the mountain, the cost would be too great. He'd felt the heat radiating off her even as she sat. She was burning hot just to remain standing. One way or another, she'd be mad by summer.

Or dead.

He couldn't help her.

But he also couldn't leave her alone.

At the very least, he could witness her end.

He followed her, his thoughts as dark as the tunnels they

passed through. She wobbled from side to side, walking almost as drunkenly as the guide who led them.

The tunnels here branched and branched again. All of them were perfectly smooth, and at each intersection, the churchman turned with perfect confidence. Tomas tracked their turns, but if they went much farther, he wasn't sure he'd be able to find his way out again.

Their descent affected him, too. Elzeth's agitation fed into his own unease, and every couple of dozen steps he had to pause to hold in his vomit.

Then their guide stopped. He turned around and smiled, baring his sharp teeth again, then gestured them forward.

Lyana passed him and stepped into a chamber beyond.

Tomas stumbled after her. Every step seemed to make his discomfort twice as bad as before. Nothing like this had ever troubled him.

When he reached the guide, he almost drew his sword to kill him. One less enemy was one less enemy. But something in the other man's posture warned Tomas that he was more than he seemed. And Tomas was hardly in the best shape to fight.

He hated putting an enemy at his back, but Lyana was too far ahead. She stood in a large chamber, torch raised above her head, sword held tightly in her other hand.

Tomas joined her, remaining a few paces behind.

In the darkness, something enormous slithered toward them.

23

The creature emerged from the shadows and into the light of Lyana's torch.

Tomas' heart skipped a beat and he took an involuntary step backward.

The beast was enormous. He guessed it was two, maybe three times the size of a man, but there was almost nothing human about it. Powerful, sinuous tentacles spread from a central torso. The limbs tumbled over one another as the creature advanced, but the torso remained steady.

Tomas barely noticed any of that.

His attention was focused on the center of the creature's body. It was one giant eye, green and reptilian, with a dark vertical slit of a pupil.

That eye was focused directly on him.

An intelligence lurked behind that gaze, something completely alien and powerful. Before it, Tomas was small and insignificant, an ant beneath the foot of a giant. The lidless eye stared at him with an intensity no human stare could match.

Lyana stood before it, torch held high.

She'd never looked so small. But her stand would have made any soldier Tomas had ever served with proud. The torch was as steady as if it was held by a statue of granite. The tip of her sword barely wobbled. If she felt any fear, he didn't see it.

Tomas' stomach clenched so hard it brought him down to a knee. Tentacles reached out toward him, but he wasn't sure he could stand, much less fight.

He'd always said the world was full of mystery, and he'd always believed it. Events regularly occurred that he couldn't explain. Those inclined toward religion saw purpose and a greater plan. Tomas saw a connected system beyond human comprehension.

This creature was more than a mystery. Its presence challenged every fundamental assumption about life he'd ever had.

It made him feel as though humanity was doomed.

That it hadn't belonged on this world in the first place.

Lyana took matters into her own hands. She tossed her torch high into the air. Well before it reached the apex of its flight, she had the tip of her broken sword aimed at the creature's eye. She leaped forward.

Tomas' only thought, lame as it was, was that he should have given her his sword, as it had a far superior edge.

Before the monster, he was no hero. He could barely summon the will to move. How Lyana acted, he couldn't explain.

Her attack lacked any technique. She possessed no balance, and her grip on the sword was awkward. But what she lacked, she more than made up for with speed and ferocity.

Lyana faced a monster, and like the monster, she didn't even blink.

Her time had come to strike the killing blow.

One of the tentacles whipped out, a blur in the darkness. It caught Lyana in the side. He heard bones crack, and her body went limp in midair. The blade clattered to the ground as she tumbled like a rag doll across the floor.

Tomas was frozen. He couldn't even will his legs to run to her aid.

The torch Lyana threw landed on the floor next to the sword. It sputtered but remained alight.

He'd barely seen the blow, and the creature had at least seven or eight of those tentacles. "Elzeth?" His request was half a question and half a plea for aid. He had no chance alone.

There was no answer.

The monster ignored Tomas, slithering and sliding toward Lyana's body. She remained perfectly motionless.

Tomas' hand went to his sword, but he didn't draw. He felt nothing but the horrible, gut-wrenching feeling of Elzeth struggling wildly against an invisible attacker. What chance did he have? His sword was meaningless.

But he had other weapons, too.

His eyes widened at the thought, then darted to the torch in his hand.

Had Elzeth been paying any attention, he would have called Tomas a fool, and he would have been right to do so. But in that moment, it was the only plan that made even a bit of sense.

Tomas stripped the pack off his back and dumped it on the floor. The creature was only a few feet away from Lyana, its tentacles growing ever closer to her prone form.

The explosive was the last object to fall out of his pack. He grabbed both sticks. Better safe than sorry, and he'd never have another chance, anyway. He lit the fuses with the fire from the torch.

The fuses burned slower than he expected. He had no experience with explosives, but the fuses gave him several seconds to realize the magnitude of his foolishness.

He didn't have any clue how strong the explosion would be.

But it didn't take much to imagine the whole cavern collapsing on top of him.

And there was no easy way out.

"Hells," he said.

The burning fuses prevented him from considering alternative ideas.

And the monster was too close to Lyana.

Tomas threw the explosive. The sticks tumbled, end over end, the burning fuses leaving circular afterimages in Tomas' vision. Both sticks landed behind the creature, so the monster's body shielded Lyana from the blast.

It wasn't enough, but it was all he could do.

The creature reacted instantly. It snapped out with its tentacles, and it flung the sticks into the far recesses of the room, a place Lyana's torch had never lit. And then the creature disappeared. No longer was it a lumbering monstrosity, but a sleek predator, slithering across the stone faster than any snake.

Tomas ran toward Lyana, sliding across the smooth floor and wrapping her in a tight embrace.

Then there was light and sound. The mountain rumbled, and then there was a crack so loud Tomas feared the world had split in two. The solid stone underneath him gave way, and there was nothing beneath him. He felt himself falling, but everything was dark. He couldn't say what was up or down.

All he could do was hold onto Lyana.

He struck water, the impact expelling what little breath he had left in his body. He sank underwater. The water churned and buffeted him, and he had a sense of motion, of being pulled.

He needed to surface, but he didn't know which way was up. Pressure assaulted his head, squeezing him from all directions.

Then his head broke water. He took a deep, gulping breath, inhaling metallic-tasting water along with precious air.

The current pulled him under again. Except for his grip on Lyana, he forced his body to relax. He didn't even know which direction to struggle toward. Better to save his strength for when it might make a difference.

His head broke the surface of the water again. He breathed, enjoying his first full breath in almost a minute. The current still pulled him rapidly along, but it no longer tumbled him like a rock in a spinning cup.

Tomas positioned Lyana so that she could breathe, too. Her body was limp. He felt for a heartbeat, but couldn't find one.

Gradually, as his hearing returned, he became aware of a dull roar. It grew louder.

Tomas swore. He kicked perpendicular to the current, but the sound quickly became deafening.

Once again, the world fell away from him, and he swore he would never take solid ground for granted again.

He maintained just enough sense to gulp one precious lungful of air before hitting the water below.

He surfaced a few seconds later. The current had largely disappeared, and he suspected they had reached some sort of pool. Again, he kicked, reaching out with one hand so that he wouldn't bump his head.

He found a stone wall.

For a while, he followed the wall, running the tips of his fingers along it. Like the tunnels above, it was smooth. Too smooth to be natural.

The current eventually grabbed him again, but this time without violence. It pulled him away from the falls. The sound of the crashing water faded.

He'd just about given up when he felt the backs of his feet scrape against something smooth. A moment later, his back brushed up against a slanted piece of stone. He pulled Lyana up it, his feet slipping as he tried to find purchase.

An inch at a time, he pulled them out of the water.

Once he was certain she was safe, he flopped onto his back next to her, staring into perfect darkness.

He had no idea where they were or how he was going to escape. Elzeth was useless. They had no supplies at all.

And he couldn't bring himself to care.

He closed his eyes and let exhaustion take him.

24

Disorientation crashed over Tomas when he woke. Whether his eyes were open or closed there was only that constant, perfect darkness. For several long seconds he didn't know if he was awake or trapped in some never-ending nightmare.

He almost wished it was the nightmare. At least then, all he'd need to do to escape was wake up.

It was the girl's breathing that convinced him he still dwelled in the land of the living. Her breaths came slow and steady, and in time he matched his breathing to hers. The slower breathing helped contain his fears.

"You there?" Tomas asked.

"I am." Elzeth didn't sound particularly pleased by the fact.

Tomas wanted to yell at the sagani. He wanted to lay the blame for everything that had happened at his feet. If they had just worked together, the scene above might have turned out much different.

The temptation died shortly after it was born. It was a familiar one. One of the benefits, and challenges, of having a companion who never left your side was that there was always somebody to pin your failures on.

There were only two problems with the approach. The first was that it simply wasn't true. If Elzeth had been able to help, he would have. Tomas didn't doubt that for a moment. Not only was Elzeth an ally, their fates were linked. If Tomas died, Elzeth did, too. Mutual interest made for a strong relationship.

The second problem was that blame served no purpose. The two of them were stuck together for the rest of their days, without so much as a chance of having a day apart. Constantly arguing over who was to blame for every mistake and failure was one of the quickest routes to a miserable existence.

So instead Tomas asked, "How are you?"

"I've had better days," the sagani answered dryly.

"You and me both."

Any discussion over what had happened could wait until they didn't have anything better to do. Right now, survival ranked quite a bit higher than reflection.

He took stock of his situation, and was unsurprised to find that he didn't like the conclusions he reached. All their supplies were lost. He couldn't see a thing. And he was with a girl who he wasn't sure he could trust. When she woke up, would she be Lyana, or something else?

On top of all of that, there was still that *thing* lurking somewhere in the caves. For all he knew, it could be hunting them right now, silently approaching just a few feet away.

He forced the thought away.

Nothing good ever happened underground.

The sound of the girl stirring ended his moping. When he heard her breathing change, he assumed she was awake. "How are you?"

She startled at the sound of his voice, but quickly calmed. That was one worry, at least, he could set aside for the moment. He remained impressed by how collected she remained, no matter their circumstances. "Where are we?"

"Not sure. Going to guess deep underground."

Lyana was silent for a moment. Then, "Have you found a way out yet?"

As if it was the most natural expectation to have.

Tomas scoffed. "Don't know if you noticed, but it's a bit dark."

"So use your hands," she replied. "You have other senses. Try using them."

Once the anger at being lectured by a girl passed, he remembered that he was here with the daughter of a prospector. In this situation, she might contribute more to their survival than he did. For all the time he'd been awake, he hadn't searched for the exit yet.

"Can you help?" he asked Elzeth.

"It doesn't matter how well you can see if there's no light to see by," the sagani replied.

"Can you, or can't you?"

Elzeth grumbled but came to life. There was a quick flash of warmth and strength, both very welcome. Then the sagani settled into a more normal state, burning gently.

Elzeth hadn't been wrong. Even with sharper senses, the blackness of the cave was absolute. But the girl hadn't been wrong either. Tomas held up his hand and felt the faintest rush of air moving past it. The girl confirmed his suspicion. "There's a gap in the wall here."

Tomas was about to suggest that she let him lead the way, but stopped. Here, he was in her domain. "You go first." He followed the sounds of her movement, and he found a slit in the cave wall. Perhaps it was a good thing that he had lost his pack. He wasn't sure that he would have fit trying to carry it. He began shuffling sideways, exploring the space in front of him with his leading hand.

Their progress was slow. After every small step or two, Tomas paused to feel the walls of the crack. To his dismay, the slit they had found grew smaller the farther in they went.

But they were committed now, and Tomas wasn't sure there was any way but forward. The walls squeezed in tight enough that he had to pull his sword from his hip and hold it with his trailing hand.

His heart began to pound. If this crack got much narrower, he'd be stuck.

Elzeth returned to his customary state of rest. The sagani cut off his protest. "Right now, me being active is the opposite of what you want. You need to relax if you want to make it through these caves."

Tomas understood the point, but it didn't make him feel any better. "Just stay close, will you?"

Elzeth didn't even give one of his customary glib responses. "I will."

Tomas had no idea how far the two of them traveled. They shuffled ever onward, but their pace was slow, and in the void they traveled through, there was no sense of time. They might've gone thirty feet or half a mile, and Tomas honestly couldn't say which. Ahead of him, Lyana grunted. She answered his question before he could even ask. "It's going to get tight," she said.

Tomas inched forward, feeling with his hands as the top of the crack came lower and lower. He had to duck lower, but there was no way to easily bend. Contorting his body into the angles required strained muscles Tomas wasn't used to using. The effort needed to move grew by the moment, and his breathing quickened.

His chest couldn't expand enough to get a full breath, and he suddenly felt an uncontrollable urge to cry.

At the sounds of his discomfort, Lyana laughed. "You can make it," she said.

He would have felt better if she'd sounded more convinced.

The ceiling continued to lower, but the crack grew wider.

Eventually, Tomas found himself on his belly crawling forward like a lizard. The space was wide enough that he could breathe more easily, but that was about it.

He hated it.

Whenever he breathed, he could feel the weight of the mountain pressing down against his back. All the mountain had to do was shift a few inches, and he'd never draw breath again.

He felt forward with his hands, then dug in his toes and inched forward. It was slow, exhausting progress. If not for the sounds of the fearless young girl in front of him, he wasn't sure he would've had the courage to continue.

The sounds of Lyana's movement came to a stop. He heard her muttering something under her breath but couldn't quite understand it. "What?"

"It's about to get a whole lot narrower," she said.

"Swell," Tomas replied.

25

"No way out but forward. No way out but forward."

Tomas whispered the words as a sort of nearly-silent mantra.

The sounds coming from ahead of him weren't promising. Lyana had slipped through the earlier cracks with ease, but the sounds of her struggling made it clear just how small of a space awaited him.

He inched forward, the stone squeezing down on him from above. It became harder and harder to breathe.

Then, without warning, there was no more space. He pushed with his toes and pulled with his fingertips, but his body didn't move. He was trying to push an oversized peg through a tiny hole, and it wasn't working.

"I'm stuck," he said.

Lyana cursed, a string of words that surprised Tomas and made him temporarily forget his predicament. It sounded as though she was coming back for him. It was the most beautiful sound he had ever heard.

He'd imagined dying in a lot of ways. But not like this.

His breath came in short, ragged gasps. When he tried to

breathe slowly through his nose to calm his terror, no air entered his lungs. The cave was tight, squeezing tighter and tighter. He imagined himself clenched in the fist of a giant. Any moment now he knew he was going to suffocate.

Something inside of him broke. Against sharpened steel or a horde of enemies, he believed he would meet his end with dignity. But this was a terror that reached beyond his conditioning and beyond his experience, seizing upon a primal fear to which he had no defense.

The mountain crushed him, unrelenting in its lack of mercy.

He cried out when a small pair of hands grabbed his own. They grasped his tightly. "You're almost there," she said. "If you can squeeze through this, you'll be safe."

She provided the first glimmer of hope felt since he'd seen the monster. It made him as grateful for her as he'd ever been for anyone in his life. But she was wrong. "I can't do it. It's too tight. You'll have to go on without me."

The girl laughed. "I've been trying to get rid of you for days, and now you're finally willing to let me leave?"

Her gentle mockery brought him to his senses faster than any encouragement would have.

Anger, it turned out, was a surprisingly effective antidote to fear.

His breathing finally slowed. He still couldn't get a full breath, but he was still with her. He was ready to try.

"We're going to work together," she said. "You're going to breathe out every bit of air you can. Then, I'm going to pull while you push. You understand?"

"I—" He didn't want to breathe all his precious air out. He was having too much trouble getting it in. There had to be a better way.

But the girl knew best. He nodded, only to remember

that she couldn't see him any more than he could see her. "I'm ready."

Lyana counted down from three, and on one, Tomas blew out what little air remained in his body. Lyana pulled, and Tomas dug his toes into the hard stone and pushed with all his might. He cried out as the stone cut through his clothes and skin, but then there was a sense of movement and he was out.

Tomas drew in one deep, shuddering breath, and the air was some of the sweetest he'd ever tasted. "Thank you."

"You can thank me once we're off this mountain."

He heard her continue on, and he followed her, the way becoming easier.

Up ahead, he saw a blue light, a familiar one. The light of Shen. He blinked, and when he looked up the light of the moon almost blinded him. He wiped the tears from his eyes, and Lyana did him the courtesy of pretending she hadn't noticed.

The crack had opened up into a cavern, and a hole taunted them, just twenty feet over their heads. But Tomas could see the climb was an easy one. He took the lead, and Lyana let him.

"Let's get out of these caves and then we can rest," he said.

She nodded, looking like she completely agreed. Despite her composure, she also seemed glad to be out of the darkness.

The climb out only took them a few minutes. Though his body was exhausted, he pulled himself up the wall faster than he believed possible. He reached the top, then turned around to offer aid to Lyana.

She summited the small wall before he could even offer his help. Together, they crawled out into the open air. They came out on a small ledge that overlooked the valley below. Tomas flopped onto his back, utterly exhausted.

Beside him, Lyana did the same. She sounded as exhausted as he felt. "Thank you for not leaving me when I told you to."

Tomas was about to tell her that those were the exact words he should be saying to her, but she was already asleep. Tomas closed his eyes with every intent of doing the same.

Of course, that was the moment Elzeth spoke up. "Can we talk?"

He groaned. "Can it wait?"

"I don't think so."

Tomas sat up so he wouldn't fall asleep. He thought he caught a glimmer of movement in the valley below, but couldn't be sure. All he wanted was to rest. "Well, talk."

"That thing we saw? I think it was a sagani."

Tomas considered it for a moment. "Suppose I can't imagine it being anything else, though I really don't know. It's not normal."

"I agree," Elzeth said. "Either something happened to it when it was born, or it somehow developed abilities I never believed possible."

"Like controlling other sagani?"

"That would be on the top of the list, yes."

Nothing Elzeth said was terribly surprising. More, it was confirmation of some of Tomas' worst fears. But it also wasn't anything that couldn't have waited until the morning. "So why the urgency?"

"Because when we were down there, it and I fought. It wanted to control me, too."

Tomas waited, certain there was more.

"While we were fighting, something between us

changed. At first, it wanted to control me the same way it controls everything. But then it learned more about us. And something in its attention shifted."

"What do you mean?"

"I think I know how the girl feels. In fact, I'm pretty sure that it wants us almost as much as it wants her."

26

Elzeth's warnings did little to stop Tomas from falling quickly asleep. He dreamed tentacled nightmares, and watched Lyana die before him in a dozen different ways, all equally terrifying. When he woke, the sun was well above the horizon and sweat dampened his clothes.

Lyana was already awake. She was sitting up, her eyes on the valley below. "Rough night?"

Tomas grunted and pushed himself to sitting.

It wasn't the best night of sleep he'd ever had, but it was rest, and he'd desperately needed it. Combined with open air and the sun on his face, hope stirred in his heart again.

They were probably still going to die.

But in the light of day, it didn't seem *quite* as likely as the night before.

Something on Lyana's cheek glinted in the morning sunlight, and when Tomas looked closer, he saw a trail of tears.

After all that she had suffered, her tears still surprised him. He hadn't seen her cry yet, and had assumed she wasn't the type. She saw that he noticed, and wiped her cheeks with the back of her hand, sniffling. "I miss him," she said.

Tomas nodded. He'd never been much good at sympathy, but he could listen. He found that more often than not, that was all people needed.

The small confession broke the dam that had been holding her emotions within. She started shaking, the tears coming freely. "I'm mad at him, too," she admitted. "I'm furious that he died and left me here alone."

She wiped her tears away again. "That's foolish, right? It's not like he was trying to die. He fought against those who came to our camp, but what chance did he have against swords and those cursed sagani? But it doesn't matter. When I think of him, I can't decide if I want to mourn his memory or punch it."

She bit down on whatever else she was about to say, and she looked away from him.

Tomas spoke softly. "It's not foolish."

Her eyes darted his way, and he elaborated. "I've seen a lot of deaths come to people in a lot of ways. There's never anything foolish about how we grieve. It's different for everyone."

His observation drew out the rest of her confession. "It's just..." She faltered. "Life was never easy for us. He tried so hard to make the best out of the hell life had become, and he always pushed himself because he wanted something more for me." She gestured to their surroundings. "It even brought us out here. He rarely spoke about it, but I know he criticized himself for not providing a better life for me. He deserved better."

Lyana cast her gaze to the sky, as if she were looking for someone above the clouds, looking back down on her. "If I had another minute with him, you know what I would tell him?"

Tomas gave a small shake of his head.

"I would tell him that he was a great man, and that nothing else mattered, so long as I knew he was there for me."

The words hooked into Tomas' heart.

He had no family he knew of, and the people he would call friends he could list on one hand with a couple of fingers left over. But his opinion was much the same as Lyana's. What one did in the world mattered a lot less than who one did it with.

Loss had granted the girl a wisdom most spent a lifetime seeking.

Her words renewed his determination. Before, he had pursued her out of some basic sense of decency. No child deserved to wander these mountains alone. It had been a vague sense of purpose, of trying to do some good in the world he'd wronged so greatly.

No longer.

Now he wanted Lyana to have a future. He wanted to see what she would do with the strength and wisdom this mountain had given her. And to see that, he needed to get her off this mountain.

The clouds blew away, and the sun shined brightly on him, warming him to the bone. "Are you still set on revenge?" he asked.

She didn't answer for several seconds. When she did, it sounded like her voice was coming from someplace far away. "I thought that if I could kill that monster, it would somehow make the world seem right again. But that's not true, is it? When I killed the man who killed my father, nothing happened. It would have been the same with the monster, right?"

Tomas nodded.

"I know he would want me to get on with living. That was all he ever wanted for me." She made a sound that was somewhere between a grunt and a chuckle. "I can even hear his voice, telling me not to worry about him. That he's fine. He was always fine."

She brushed some imaginary dust off her legs. "Thank you, for everything."

"You can thank me when we get off this mountain."

"It will be looking for both of us. When we were down there, I felt its attention on you, too."

The confirmation of Elzeth's suspicion didn't make Tomas feel any better, but it didn't change their situation much. One way or the other, pursuit was pretty much inevitable. At least now, he wouldn't have to worry about Lyana's motives. "I felt the same," Tomas admitted. "So let's get off this mountain as quick as we can."

Lyana grimaced. "I think I need food."

Tomas had worried about that. "Does it hurt?"

"A lot."

Not only had she gone through the evolution, she'd been dealing with injuries, exhaustion, and cold. He was a little surprised she wasn't eating her own arm.

They needed food, and as far as he'd seen, there wasn't any game on this haunted mountain. "Do you think you could make it back down to Tatum's?"

"I can try."

"I need you to be honest. Can you?"

She shook her head. "It's going to be hard to even walk."

There was only one place on this mountain where he'd

seen food. "We need to go back to the camp where the miners were. They have food brought to them."

"It's surrounded by sagani. They'll know where we are."

"Then we should try to have a plan by the time we get there."

Lyana laughed. "You don't strike me as a person who's very good at making plans."

The girl really was too clever for her own good. "Then let me rephrase. Perhaps you'll have a good plan by the time we get there."

He stood and stretched. He'd managed his own energy better than her, but it wouldn't be long before his need for food became a problem, too. He offered her his hand and helped her to her feet. Though the movement appeared smooth enough, he felt the tension through her grip. He didn't say anything, but he worried.

She didn't have much time.

27

T heir progress across the mountain was agonizingly slow.

Lyana struggled to put one foot in front of the other. Tomas spent most of his time searching for hostile sagani. They had made themselves scarce, though. For the first time in days, they seemed to have the mountain to themselves. Tomas didn't question his luck. He only wished Lyana could move faster.

He could have made his life easier by simply hiding Lyana away. But he feared leaving her alone for long. The way this week had been going, the moment he left her would be the moment a sagani found her. In her current state, she couldn't even swing a stick.

Fortunately, their journey into the mountain hadn't carried them as far away from the camp as Tomas would have guessed when they wandered the absolute darkness. The camp was on the east side of the mountain, and the cave they had climbed out of was on the southeast face. If he'd had the ability to fly, the journey wouldn't have taken more than a few minutes.

Even stuck to the ground, alone, it wouldn't have taken more than an hour.

With Lyana in tow, it was afternoon by the time they neared the campsite.

Though it slowed their progress, Tomas elected to climb higher the closer they came to their destination. He wanted the view, but he also suspected more sagani roamed the woods than the rock above. They hadn't seen any sagani all day, and on this mountain, that was worth noting.

Tomas picked his way carefully across the mountain. Behind him, Lyana swayed as she walked, and there were a few places where he feared she would stumble down the steep slope. She accepted his support without complaint as they passed particularly treacherous sections.

Despite her obvious suffering, he felt no heat from her at those times.

Sagani granted humans incredible strength, but they presented a constant temptation. The power was always there, just a thought away. Whatever the problem, it felt right to utilize the sagani.

But the temptation was a trap.

The longer Tomas lived as a host, the more convinced he was that the less a host used the sagani, the healthier they remained. In Lyana's predicament, using her sagani would have eased the pain and given her the strength to walk faster. It would have started to eat her alive, and she would burn faster, racing ahead of the pain, creating a negative cycle that would have ended with her mad and emaciated.

Just like the residents of the camp they approached. Like most of the hosts Tomas had crossed paths with for years.

He knew many who would have given in long ago. Fighting that temptation would be the biggest, most important battle of her life. And it would only end when she traveled to the gate.

That was the double-edged sword of becoming a host. The choice she'd been too young to make.

When they neared the camp, Tomas found a cleft in the rocks where Lyana could hide. He clasped her hand between his. "I'll be back with food. It might take me a while. Don't leave."

She smiled weakly. "Don't think I'll be running anytime soon."

"And don't burn. You understand that, right?"

She nodded and closed her eyes. "Don't worry about me. I'll be right here waiting for you."

"I'll be back as soon as I can."

He wished there was something more he could say, but nothing mattered. She looked like she would be asleep in a few minutes. He didn't want to leave her here, unattended and asleep, but there were no better choices.

He took one last look at her, then stepped away.

Now that he was alone, he climbed even higher, putting as much distance between him and her as he could. The closer he came to the camp, the more likely it was he would be spotted. He didn't want to lead the sagani to her.

Ten minutes of hiking brought him to a small outcropping of rocks that overlooked the camp. From his position he could look down both on the tents and on the trail that led to the cave.

The camp was silent, and Tomas assumed the hosts were in the cave, working on whatever task the monster had assigned them. Unfortunately, the camp appeared to be empty of food as well. The deer from yesterday was gone.

He settled in to wait.

Most of the afternoon passed before Tomas saw movement down below. The spider-shaped sagani came, carrying a clutch of hares between them. Tomas' mouth watered as the sagani dropped the dead creatures in the center of the camp.

The spiders left as quickly as they had come. Tomas waited a few minutes, watching the edges of the clearing like a hawk waiting for a meal. He saw no movement.

"Now, or if we get in trouble?" he asked.

Elzeth debated for a moment. "Now." He woke, stirring just enough for Tomas to shake off the exhaustion that had settled deep in his muscles. Tomas barely noticed the brief flare-up that came before. "You're getting better at this."

Elzeth wasn't in a mood to talk. "Get moving. If it's like last time, it won't be long before those other hosts make an appearance."

Tomas didn't need to be told twice. He picked his way down the mountainside, relishing the ease of movement Elzeth afforded him. Within two minutes they were in the clearing. Tomas went to the tents first.

He needed two tries, but he found one of the well-organized tents and looted it quickly. He found a pack with cooking essentials, and a waterskin. The materials were more precious than gold. Tomas dumped out everything else, then ran over to where the sagani had dropped off the hares. He grabbed them all and stuffed them in the pack. He could almost smell them roasting over a fire.

A quick glance around the campsite didn't reveal anything else useful. If he wanted, he supposed he could steal a tent, but the risk was too great for too little benefit. It never hurt to sleep under the stars.

He heard the hosts long before they were in view. Their shuffling steps kicked loose stone down the path. It was time to go.

Just as he was about to run, another sound caught his attention. To the east, a lone sagani came out of the woods. It looked straight at him, and Tomas swore.

He ran south, and the sagani pursued, its feet skittering across the rock as it kept pace. Above him, he heard the pace of the hosts increase. They knew he was there, and they were coming for him.

Tomas ran faster, and all the predators on the mountain gave chase.

28

The flaw in Tomas' strategy quickly became apparent. No matter how fast he fled, he couldn't outrun everything hunting him on this mountain. Hells, he couldn't outrun a single sagani. He slowed to a stop.

He needed a moment to think.

The footsteps of the miners grew closer and louder, only a few hundred feet behind.

Elzeth and Lyana both believed the creature at the heart of the mountain wanted them. Tomas assumed that meant alive. That had to give him an advantage. In his experience, the side most willing to kill the other side usually won.

Unless they were dramatically outnumbered.

The footsteps thundered in his hearing. Clumsy as they were, the miners sounded like a group twice as large as their actual number.

No brilliant ideas came to mind. There was a reason he'd never become an officer in the war. Put a sword in his hands and he was as strong a warrior as most anyone on the field. But tactics and strategy were beyond him.

He'd become a master of choosing between two options: either run from his problems or attack them ferociously.

Running wasn't getting him anywhere useful.

Tomas drew his sword and turned to face the hosts.

"Wondered how long it would be before you settled on that," Elzeth said, completely unsurprised.

Tomas charged the men pursuing him.

In most circumstances, attacking so many hosts was as quick a suicide as he knew. But these weren't hosts in full control of their bodies or powers. The creature's control was far from perfect.

As one, the hosts came to a stop. None of them were armed with anything beyond a pickax. Tomas cut the leader down before he even reacted.

The old man's murder jolted the rest of them to action. They scattered, quick as any deer bounding away from a predator. Tomas chose one at random and pursued. The prospector had the edge in speed. He burned hotter than Tomas dared. His movements, though, lacked any semblance of grace. He hit a tree, which spun him around and gave Tomas a chance to catch him.

Tomas led with his fist, punching the prospector as hard in the stomach as he could. The host doubled over, and in a moment, Tomas was behind him, yanking his head back and holding the edge of his sword against the man's neck.

He needed a hostage more than he needed a victim.

The prospector went still. The forest quieted as his partners also came to a stop.

"Tell it to leave us alone, or I keep killing its help."

"You do remember we don't have a spoken language, right?" Elzeth asked.

"Just try."

Tomas felt the stirring in his stomach as Elzeth gathered

himself. The sagani spoke without words, making Tomas' intent clear. The communication tickled the edges of Tomas' awareness, a mixture of sight, sound, and feeling. He spoke to the sagani within the prospector, and hopefully, to the monster who controlled the sagani.

Elzeth continued for several heartbeats, then fell silent, the stirring in Tomas' stomach fading. The others made no immediate response.

Then, one by one, the hosts retreated to their camp. The spider-like sagani that had first spotted him in the clearing remained. Elzeth spoke again, and it, too, disappeared.

When Tomas was certain they were alone, he released his grip on the host's hair and removed the sword from his neck. He took a step back.

The host turned and stared at him with blank eyes, then also began shuffling back to camp.

Tomas let out a long sigh of relief. "Think it worked?"

"Doubt it. It'll try something else. Or wait until you've dropped your guard."

Tomas glanced up the mountain. "How smart do you think it is?"

"Not very, actually. Just smart enough to be dangerous."

Tomas considered that. Maybe it gave them an edge, but if so, he didn't know how to take advantage of it. "Let's get this food to Lyana before it's too late."

Tomas ran, his footsteps light through the trees. Nothing followed him that he noticed. But just to be safe, before turning back up the mountain, he clambered up a tree. Once he was twenty feet in the air, he found a branch to rest on and waited.

A few minutes later, one of the sagani appeared. It came from the same direction as Tomas, its limbs almost silent as it skittered closer to Tomas' perch.

The sagani stopped and looked around, then continued on its way. Tomas breathed slowly as it passed underneath the tree. He craned his neck so he could watch the sagani leave. The creature walked on, still searching, giving no clue that it had spotted Tomas.

"I get the feeling it's not going to let us go so easily," Tomas said.

When the sagani was well out of sight, Tomas descended the tree. He suspected that before long the area would be crawling with creatures searching for him. He gathered some dry wood for a fire and walked straight up the mountain.

His sharpened senses caught sight of another sagani approaching. He ducked behind a wide tree, hoping he hadn't been spotted.

The sagani seemed in no hurry. It would walk a dozen paces, then stop and look around. As it neared, Tomas imagined himself becoming one with the wide pine. The sagani passed about twenty feet away on the other side of the tree, stopping and searching the whole time.

While he waited, Tomas studied the rocks above. Once he broke from the trees, there wouldn't be much in the way of cover.

But no sagani wandered the rocks.

Tomas couldn't guess why. The spider shape that most of the sagani took in this area were certainly capable of climbing. If anything, they were ideally made for it.

When he was certain he was out of sight of the searching sagani, he broke from cover at a run. He sprinted through the last of the trees and into the rocks. He found a boulder to crouch behind, and he looked back into the trees.

More than anything, he couldn't afford to give away

Lyana's position. There was nothing he could do if they found her.

The woods were silent. No sagani chased him, nor could he see any moving among the trees.

When he was sure that he was unobserved, Tomas picked his way higher. Thanks to Elzeth, the journey wasn't nearly as long or arduous as it could have been. Before long he was on familiar territory, and he hurried to find Lyana.

He reached the place where he'd left her, and he stopped in his tracks.

He looked around.

He was sure this was where he had left her.

But she wasn't here.

29

Tomas' hand went to his sword.

He put the wood he carried down, ready for whatever fresh danger awaited him.

"Lyana?" He spoke softly, not wanting his voice to carry. He walked past the cleft where he had left her, searching for any clue that would reveal what had happened or where she had gone.

His search revealed nothing. He found no tracks on the stone, nor did he find any signs of a struggle. There was no blood, no clumps of hair, no scraps of fabric.

"Lyana?" He called a little louder, and this time, small stones tumbled down the slope half a dozen paces ahead of him. The sound drew his eyes upward, where the rocks jutted outward and blocked his line of sight.

He scrambled higher and found Lyana behind the boulder, her arms hugging her knees tightly into her chest. When she raised her head, he saw tears in her eyes. "I can't resist much longer," she said. "I know it will make the pain go away."

Tomas knelt beside her. "Why are you up here?"

But Lyana had retreated deep within and couldn't hear him. She fought a battle against herself, and it was only a matter of time before she lost. The fact she'd lasted this long spoke volumes about the strength of her will.

Tomas picked her up as gently as he would a newborn, surprised again by how easy it was. If she went much longer without food, the clothes she wore would weigh more than she did. He picked his way carefully down the slope, returning to the cleft where he'd left the firewood.

Once she was nestled safely within the crack, Tomas prepared the food he'd stolen. The fire caught quickly, and as it burned down to coals, he skinned and gutted the animals. He worked fast, cutting the meat into smaller pieces that would cook faster.

Lyana barely moved. She remained tightly balled in a fetal position, curled in on herself.

As he worked, he kept glancing down the mountain to the woods below. The fire ruined his vision, but he saw nothing crawling toward them.

It was about time they had a bit of luck.

Tomas had the first cuts of meat ready in record time. He couldn't speak to the taste, but he'd long believed hunger was the best seasoning.

By that standard, Lyana was about to feast on the greatest meal she'd ever tasted.

He handed the food to her, but she didn't even notice. Tomas grimaced, then grabbed one of the cuts and brought it to her lips. As soon as the meat made contact, she nearly bit his fingers off in her rush to eat it.

She devoured the bite in a few heartbeats.

The transformation that came over her made her into a new person. Her arms relaxed and her eyes opened. The fire within them returned. A smile grew on her face as she looked at all the food still cooking over the fire. That grin told him all he needed to know.

She'd been fighting a losing battle, a lone warrior surrounded on all sides by overwhelming temptations. Tomas had arrived with reinforcements just as all hope seemed lost.

He took a little for himself, but left most of the meat for Lyana.

"Thank you," she said.

He gave her a small bow of acknowledgment, and asked the question that had been worrying him since he returned. "Why weren't you here?"

"I thought I heard someone moving below. I figured if it was you, you'd go straight to where I was, but this person was wandering back and forth. So I climbed a bit higher to hide. I meant to return, but..." Her voice trailed off, and she seemed ashamed by her weakness.

"You resisted longer than most would have, and on this mountain, that's worth even more."

Her cheeks flushed briefly, and she changed the topic. "What do we do next?"

Tomas looked down the mountain. Tolkin lit the plains far below with its pale red light. They were so close to freedom and still so far away. "I'm not sure," he confessed. "I don't know how to get off this mountain, but I really don't want to cross paths with that monster again."

"Is there a way to sneak away without being spotted?"

"Unlikely. The forest below seems to be crawling with sagani. And we only need to be spotted once."

"What about going over the mountain?" Lyana pointed west.

Tomas blinked rapidly, and Elzeth rumbled with laughter. "Girl's smarter than you," he said.

He'd been thinking of the mountain range as some sort of impassable wall, where the only way to safety was to travel back east. Lyana destroyed his assumptions with a single question. It was possible all the sagani were clustered entirely in the woods, leaving the west wide open.

Perhaps their best retreat was to advance farther into unknown territory.

"It's risky," he said. "There's no telling if we'll be able to find food, or if the sagani are there. And if we're wrong, we're even farther away from help."

"Doomed if we do, doomed if we don't," she said.

The phrase made him smile. "I once knew a man who said that all the time."

"Who was he?"

"An officer I served under in the war."

"Did you like being a soldier?"

"Sometimes. There are parts I miss. Some I don't."

She leaned back against the stone, still eating slowly. Between bites she said, "Pa and I crossed paths with a fair number of people like you. You all have the same look." She started on some of the entrails Tomas had prepared. "Pa used to say it was like you all had one foot in the past and one foot in a future that would never exist."

"Wise man."

"Sometimes. Sometimes not. But he usually had a good sense of people. Said it came from being wronged so many times." She finished off the entrails and started on another slice of meat. "So, what brings you out here?"

"Just looking for a quiet place to settle. Someplace away from people."

Lyana smiled, as though he'd told a joke.

"What?"

She shook her head, but relented at his stare. "I made

the journey out here with Pa. If all you were looking for was a quiet place to settle, you could have stopped anywhere in the last three hundred miles."

Tomas' protest died on his lips. He thought about her comment, hearing the echo of Tatum's observation in her own. "Why do *you* think I'm out here?"

She shrugged. "No idea. But I don't think it's solitude you're looking for." She finished up the last of her meal and wiggled deeper into the crack. "Think I'm going to sleep for a bit. You mind?"

"Not at all. I'll do the same myself, soon enough."

He'd barely finished speaking when he heard her snoring, the sound softly echoing in the small crack.

Tomas added the last of the wood to the fire and leaned back against a rock. The stars marched slowly overhead, the same as every other night. Clouds gathered above the peaks, and he wondered if they'd have rain soon.

He felt Elzeth, discontent and active. The way it felt, they had the same things in mind.

"Too clever for her own good," Elzeth muttered.

Tomas grunted.

The fire died down, and Tomas was about to fall asleep when he heard the soft footsteps of someone approaching. He stood, drew his sword, and went to meet their visitor.

It was the churchman, his eyes glittering with the reflected light of the fading fire. His hands were extended wide, and Tomas saw no visible weapon. "I just came to talk."

The smarter idea seemed to be to run his blade through the man, but Tomas wasn't sure he wanted to experience the consequences of that. He relented. "Say your piece."

The churchman didn't answer for a moment, and Tomas almost asked Elzeth for help. The situation smelled of a trap, and he wanted sharper senses to detect anyone else in the vicinity.

The visitor cleared his throat. "I have an offer for you. A chance for freedom."

"I'm listening."

The man shook his head. "Tomorrow. Bring the girl to my camp. It's something you both need to hear. We can break our fasts together, and you can listen to what I have to say."

"Where's your camp?"

"Keep traveling around the south side of the mountain. A little past where I suspect you two emerged earlier today. You can't miss it."

"Why should I trust you?"

The man smiled. "It's not about trust. It's the easiest way to get what I want, and the only way for you to get off this mountain alive. We all win."

Tomas didn't have to think about it long. It wasn't like he had better ideas. And if promising the man he would visit guaranteed him a restful night of sleep, he would take it.

"I'll talk to her in the morning. We'll try to be there."

The stranger offered a short bow, then disappeared into the dark.

30

By the time Tomas awoke early in the morning, storm clouds had moved in and the wind had picked up. He yawned, stretched, and cast a wary eye toward the sky. Firsthand experience had taught him the dangers of sudden weather changes, and he didn't care to be trapped on the exposed face of the mountain if a storm came through.

Lyana woke soon after him, and he told her about their evening visitor. She formed her own opinion quickly. "I don't trust him."

"I don't either, but that doesn't mean it isn't our best option."

"I'd rather try for the west side of the mountain first."

Tomas eyed the thick clouds. The idea had been a wishful dream the night before. If the weather turned on them, the journey might be the decision that killed them. "I'd rather fight humans than nature."

"We don't lose anything by trying," Lyana argued. "He's told us where his camp is, and we can always go there if something stops us."

"Any opinions?" Tomas asked Elzeth.

"She's right," Elzeth said. "It's worth the try, and if we can avoid a fight, all the better."

"You're no help."

"You just don't like losing an argument to a child," came the retort.

"Also true."

Tomas let out an exaggerated sigh. He'd been outvoted. "Let's get going, then."

They packed up what little they had. To avoid the churchman's camp, they chose to circle the mountain around the north face. Tomas led the way.

Under different circumstances, he would have dropped down a few hundred feet to the forest. From there, the mountain sloped gently upward to a saddle between two peaks. However, Tomas figured there were dozens of sagani crawling around down there, and if they tried to take the easy route, they would encounter an impassable wall of the creatures soon enough.

He didn't mind, though. He'd much rather struggle against the elevation and uneven footing than the sagani.

The rain Tomas feared arrived soon enough. He watched as a light gray wall of clouds enveloped the peak and moved down the slope. A few stray drops ricocheted off the rocks before him, and then he was in the cloud. Visibility dropped until he could only see twenty feet in front of him, and the air developed a sudden chill.

The storm held little violence, though. The rain misted gently around them, caressing their exposed skin and soaking the ground. Their footing, already worrisome, became treacherous. Tomas frequently bent over, spreading his weight between hands and feet for more stability.

The shower transformed Lyana once again. It washed

the dirt and grime that had accumulated on her clothes and in her hair. She smiled as she turned her face up to the rain.

They picked their way up and around the mountain. It wasn't the straightest or fastest path away from the danger, but at least their progress was consistent. As in their earlier travels, Lyana didn't utter a word of complaint, and she kept his pace without difficulty. She didn't even whine about the rain.

Tomas' only worry about her was how long she could maintain her strength. She had to be on the tail end of her evolution, but she still had eaten too little food for too long. The girl needed a proper feast, and soon.

The rain stopped mid-morning, but the sun didn't fight through the clouds until near noon. When the first rays struck him, he stopped, spread his arms, and basked in the short-lived warmth. As the day progressed, the sun burned more of the clouds away.

They reached the saddle not long after noon, and Tomas enjoyed his first look at the land to the west. Majestic peaks stretched off into the distance. It was a land of high summits and low valleys, and even from his vantage point, he couldn't see how far it stretched.

One fact was clear. He was nowhere near the edge of this land.

What was on the other side of those mountains? A sea? Open prairie? Or something even stranger, beyond his limited imagination?

He stared west for a good while. His reverie was interrupted when Lyana loudly cleared her throat. Her sharp eyes studied him. "You really just want to keep going west, don't you?"

"What do you think is out there?"

Her gaze followed his own. "Don't know, don't really care."

Her answer ruined his mood. It was the same answer most gave. Who cared about the mysteries of the world when survival was all that mattered?

He understood well enough. Once he might have even said the same. But after becoming a host and fighting in a war, his priorities shifted.

The unexplored western frontier called to him. It beckoned for him to enter, to wander, to discover. He shrugged. "Someday, I want to find out what's out there."

"Not enough strange and mysterious events in these parts?"

He let her snide remark slide off him. Strangers doubting his curiosity, and his sanity, wasn't a new experience. He let his eyes drop to the more immediate vicinity.

The mountain sloped down and away at a relatively gentle angle. There was a bit of a valley between this peak and the ones beyond, though its elevation was much higher than the lands to the east Tomas had come from. Pine trees grew in the valley, and Tomas traced a path south that looked passable. The girl's plan could work.

They made their way down the slope. The passing showers had made the rock slick, and Tomas had to caution Lyana about scampering down the mountain too fast.

He understood her hurry, though. They had a path. Though true escape may take another day, the end of their journey was at hand. He wanted to run down the slope, too.

As they neared the small forest, Tomas kept his eyes focused on the trees. Everything hinged on a lack of sagani on the western face, and so far, Tomas didn't see anything that worried him. Their luck just needed to hold for a bit longer.

They were both walking fast as they came to the outskirts of the forest, eager to put anything solid between them and the mountain.

From deep in the shadows, a figure emerged. The old churchman looked at them with a mischievous smile on his face. He looked up to the sky, judging the position of the sun.

"It's a little later than I prefer to break my fast," he said. "But I'm glad you're here to join me."

Four of the spider-like sagani emerged from the woods.

Tomas and Lyana couldn't refuse the invitation.

31

As before, there was something about the man before them that set the hairs on Tomas' arms standing straight up. To look at him was to observe the very definition of kindness. He had just enough of a stomach to appear harmless, and his neatly trimmed gray beard softened the angular edges of his jaw. The smile on his face matched the twinkle in his eye, making him seem like a man who knew all of life was a joke, and he was waiting for the rest of humanity to figure it out, too.

And yet, there was something more, a darkness deeply submerged under layers of kindness and hospitality. Tomas couldn't point to a single detail as evidence of his suspicion, but it didn't change his certainty.

The old man walked over to patch of grass, unslung his pack, and sat down. He moved easily, as though his body was made of light. He opened his pack and began pulling out enough food to feast on for days.

The food didn't diminish Tomas' concerns, but it did convince him to stay and hear the man out.

The spider-like sagani took up positions in a wide circle

around the group, reminding Tomas he didn't have as much choice as he liked to believe. Lyana remained close by his side as he sat across from the man.

"Name's Colvin," the man said as he brought out yet more food.

"Tomas."

"Lyana." She said her name as though it were a challenge. The fire in her eyes burned, and all her hate was focused on the churchman.

Colvin ignored Lyana's glare for the moment. He spread his hands wide. "Eat. I can only imagine how hungry you both are."

Tomas reached over and grabbed some of the dried meat before Lyana could do something foolish. Enemy or not, they needed the meal. She held out for a bit after Tomas started eating, then conceded to her own hunger.

Tomas gave Colvin a small bow, which Colvin returned in equal measure.

"Food tastes better, when one has seen death, doesn't it?"

Lyana tensed, and Colvin seemed to realize how disturbing his statement sounded. "I apologize. I meant it more as an observation. Food is life, and all things are made more poignant by their opposites. We understand good because of evil. Day because of night."

At the expressions on their faces, the smile faded a bit from his face. He looked east, to the mountain peak. "I must apologize again, I guess. It has been some time since I've met strangers, and my own death draws near. The gate makes philosophers of us all, I suppose."

"You're dying?" Tomas asked.

Colvin waved the question away. "It doesn't matter."

Tomas frowned, but Colvin didn't give him a chance to inquire further. "You know I'm a host?"

Tomas nodded. "You don't seem terribly upset about it, considering your beliefs."

Colvin looked down to the blood-red symbol on his chest. "The world is full of mysteries and wonders, and the human heart is the greatest of these."

Tomas grabbed another strip of meat. However this ended, he could ensure it wasn't on an empty stomach.

"However, this isn't really about me," Colvin said. "It's about her."

Lyana bared her teeth.

"Say your piece," Tomas said.

"I know you've met the sagani that lives under the mountain. And you," he gestured toward Tomas, "have some idea of how unique a creature it is."

"He's got your gift for understatement," Elzeth remarked.

Colvin hesitated, and then words poured from his lips. "It is the answer to every question I've ever had. I believe it is the culmination of my faith's philosophy. That creature has shown me truths that I have been seeking my whole life."

Tomas, through an incredible effort, kept the surprise on his face limited to his mouth dropping open. It took him several seconds to regain his composure. "What truths?"

"The ones that matter. Why we are here? What are the sagani? Why does this world even exist?"

"So it's shown you the answers to *everything*." Tomas couldn't keep the skepticism out of his voice.

"Hardly. Only the questions that matter."

"And you still wear that symbol?"

Colvin glanced down again, tugging at his clothes so he could see them better. When he looked back up, his smile was wide. "They're warm, and I no longer believe the sagani are categorically evil. As our society advances, so must our beliefs."

Tomas grunted. "The last churchman I met who became a host was a knight commander. Forced himself to become one to fight me. He hated himself for all the remaining moments of his life."

"So why am I not the same?" Tomas thought he saw a flash of regret in the other man's eyes, but it was suppressed a heartbeat later. Colvin helped himself to some of his own food. Lyana had lost all her hesitancy, and the meal disappeared at an alarming rate. Colvin shrugged. "At first, I was. Like all on this mountain that you've met, I did not become a host by choice. It wasn't until it revealed the truth to me that my opinion changed."

"How did it reveal this truth?"

"In visions."

Lyana scoffed. "You're a mad old man."

Tomas wanted to remind her he was a mad old man who had the cooperation of several sagani, but there was no need. Colvin turned to her. "You, of all people, deny the truth? Him, I expect to doubt. He was not made by this mountain. You were. I know you've seen the same."

Her answering silence told Tomas that Colvin was right.

"What kind of visions?" Tomas asked. "What do you know?"

Colvin shook his head. "The answers aren't mine to give." His attention was fully on Lyana now. "It wants the girl."

"Why?" Tomas asked.

Lyana surprised him by answering. "To walk the world."

She spoke as one who had known the answer for a while.

Colvin spoke directly to Lyana. "Will you?"

Lyana shook her head.

"I know that you're scared," Colvin said. "But you're more than halfway there already. And it sent me to you for a reason. So you can see that there is nothing to fear. I'm still very much myself." Colvin gestured to Lyana. "And if he comes with, there is even less to fear. It seeks to learn from him."

Tomas' gaze darted between the two of them. He suddenly felt as though he was the outsider, the enemy that needed to be defeated.

Lyana cast her eyes down.

He refused to believe she had misled him this whole time. But the longer she remained silent, the more he feared he was wrong.

Lyana's posture stiffened. "Let him go. And I will come with you without a fight."

Tomas almost choked on the piece of meat he was chewing. "Ly—"

She cut him off with a sharp gesture.

Colvin shook his head. "I'm sorry, but I can't. It needs to know the secrets Tomas carries."

"He's already taught them to me," Lyana said. "I am all that it needs."

Colvin considered that for a moment. "You're in no position to bargain."

Lyana grinned viciously, as though she'd been expecting just that answer. "On the contrary." She pulled out her knife, but before either Colvin or Tomas could react, she held it to her own throat. "If it wants me, it needs to let Tomas go."

Colvin thought about it for a few moments longer. Then he nodded. "Very well."

He began packing up the meal he'd brought, and Tomas

watched, feeling very much like he'd become an observer of a drama whose plot he didn't understand.

Colvin stood, and Lyana joined him. She turned to Tomas. "Thank you for all you've done." Her voice was strong, but Tomas saw how her eyes watered. "Now, please leave." She bowed deeply to him, her form impeccable.

And then they turned toward the mountain and left him behind.

32

Tomas watched the two figures leave, accompanied by the four sagani.

Lyana never looked back.

"Do you have any idea what just happened?" Tomas asked.

"Not the slightest," Elzeth said. "But if I had to guess, I'd say Lyana just saved our lives."

Tomas nodded. "I got that feeling, too. I thought I was supposed to be saving her."

"I've noticed your plans don't seem to work out around her very often."

Tomas grunted. He put his hands on his hips and looked around. "What do you think?"

"I don't suppose you'd consider finally leaving this mountain?"

Tomas looked south. The path called to him, promising him safety at last. "You know, just once, I'd love to *want* to make the wise choice."

"You and me both."

"I don't feel good about letting her sacrifice herself on our behalf."

"Me neither."

The forest of trees to the west was quiet, but it was a silence Tomas didn't trust. "Think we're being watched?"

"I would, if our positions were reversed."

"Think it will really let us go?"

"I have my doubts. I suspect it doesn't want much attention on whatever is happening here."

Tomas agreed. "South, then double-back tonight?"

"Why not?"

Tomas gave one last look at departing figures, now a ways away. He gave a wave for the benefit of whatever audience he might have, then turned south.

Tomas moseyed. In an hour he barely covered a mile. After the past few days of strenuous travel, the change of pace suited him. He let himself enjoy the sight of snow-capped peaks. He welcomed the cool breeze, and the eerie silence allowed him time with his thoughts.

They wouldn't have impressed any philosophers.

Mostly he worried about the headstrong girl. He hoped nothing happened to her before he returned.

He halted late in the afternoon to sit and eat some more of the food Colvin had so generously provided. While he ate, he planned.

Tracking the girl over the rocky terrain would be next to impossible. She wouldn't expect rescue, so would leave nothing to aid him. But he knew her destination, roughly. Her path ended in the heart of the mountain, face to face with that monster.

He just had to find his own way there.

Would have been convenient if the beast came out of the

mountain so that Tomas wouldn't have to go back in, but he knew his luck wasn't that good.

They came for him as soon as the sun was down.

Tomas was waiting. Elzeth blazed to life, and Tomas was on his feet as the first of the spider-like sagani came into view. It leaped at him, hooked legs slashing at his face. Tomas cut it out of the air and moved on to the next.

Without the trees to use for cover and maneuvering, the spiders weren't difficult to deal with. They attacked straight on, and Tomas dispatched them one after another. Within moments, four of them lay dead at his feet.

Killing sagani had never been so easy. Whatever they gained in coordination, they lost in individual ability. Most sagani terrified him. These barely counted as an annoyance.

Tomas searched the area quickly for signs of any others, but the night had returned to perfect stillness.

He ran back toward the mountain, his loping pace one he'd perfected over his years of travel with Elzeth. Fast enough to eat up the miles, but slow enough that he would arrive at his destination ready to fight.

He angled toward the east.

Colvin had told him the night before that his camp would be easy to find. Tomas hoped that was true.

If Colvin served the creature in the manner Tomas suspected, it stood to reason he would have a camp somewhere with access to the interior of the mountain.

An assumption, perhaps, but one that did no harm. If he didn't find an entry there, he could continue to comb the mountain, or he could run back to the eastern slopes and follow the mine that the other hosts built.

Tolkin rose, casting its red light over the slope of the mountain, and Tomas saw the camp off in the distance. An enormous tent had been built, visible for miles. He turned in that direction.

Twice he heard or saw sagani patrolling the area between him and the mountain. But he didn't get the feeling he was expected. Both times he was able to hide before he was spotted, and the patrols passed by without noticing him.

Once he found himself tangled in the thick brush, but otherwise he made good time. By the time Tolkin was high in the sky, Tomas was looking down on the camp. It appeared abandoned, but in good order.

He watched for several minutes before creeping into it.

The place was well-provisioned. Colvin must have brought several horses up here, although there was no evidence of the creatures now. Given how satiated Tomas currently felt, he suspected he had a good idea of what had become of the beasts.

He helped himself to more food as he explored. There were pickaxes and shovels, an axe and a whetstone. Nothing terribly interesting.

Tomas slipped into the tent, tall enough that he could stand and walk around without having to duck his head. A rack held one rifle, with spaces for three more that were currently empty.

That, by itself, told Tomas a great deal about Colvin.

He hadn't been some random churchman out here in the wild, though Tomas hadn't thought that for a minute after meeting him. He was somebody in the church structure. Those rifles would cost a small fortune.

There were two cots in the room, one on each of the western corners. Both had been neatly made. Tomas peeked underneath them, but found little of interest. He found no maps, no journals, no notes of any kind that might shed some light on the mysteries of this mountain.

He stepped outside the tent and looked up the slope. As he'd hoped, a trail ran up from the camp to a dark hole in the side of a granite face.

Tomas suppressed the shudder that ran through his body. The memories of his last experience in the caves were still fresh in his mind.

He found a pair of torches lying around the camp, picked them up, and hiked up the trail.

"It's getting hard to hold back," Elzeth said. "The closer we get, the more active I want to be. It's worse than before. I think something is happening in there."

"Just do what you can," Tomas replied. "One way or another, this ends tonight."

He reached the mouth of the cave and lit one of the two torches.

So long as he had light, his courage remained.

He took a deep breath.

What were the odds he'd get trapped underground again?

He slipped into the cave, torch held aloft, hoping he was ready for whatever waited for him below.

33

This cave, like the cave he and Lyana had discovered earlier, quickly transformed into a tunnel shaped by human hands. Jagged rock had been chiseled away, and thin cracks had been enlarged and reinforced by thick trunks of pine. The work here was more extensive than the work outside the other camp.

Tomas assumed this tunnel was the original, but he supposed other explanations were possible.

Though the passages were wide enough, Tomas' heart pounded harder in his chest, and he couldn't help but keep glancing up. He'd been born to roam under open skies, not tunnel under mountains.

Humans didn't belong here.

"What is it about caves you don't like?" Elzeth asked.

"No good reason. Just don't like them."

"Were you left in the dark too long as a child? Buried in sand by a mean student?"

The corner of Tomas' mouth turned up in a smile. He knew the mocking was meant to focus his thoughts elsewhere, and he appreciated it. "If I was, I don't remember it."

He thought of Lyana and her ease in the dark and tight spaces. No doubt she was used to such environments, but he wondered if she'd always been so comfortable, or if she had overcome her own early fears. The thought of her inspired him to hurry.

The cave was as silent as the forests that surrounded the mountain. He only heard the soft sounds of his passage and the occasional drip of water leaking from the rock.

The tunnel split several hundred paces into the mountain. So long as Tomas' sense of direction hadn't been destroyed by the journey, one tunnel curved to the west and one to the east. "Best guess?" he asked.

"The one to the east is likely to meet up with the tunnels we entered first."

Tomas had been thinking the same. It felt like that side of the mountain had received more attention. He took that tunnel.

Soon, his guess bore fruit. The sound of the miners working the tunnel reached his ears. Though it was the sound of enemies nearby, Tomas welcomed the noise. They were something solid. Something he understood.

Something he could cut.

He proceeded cautiously, remembering the tricks sound had played on him during his last visit. It did the same here, loud one moment and nearly impossible to hear the next.

When he finally found the hosts, though, he saw that his caution was unnecessary. Light ahead warned him he was getting close. Not long after, he poked his head around a bend and saw them. All the hosts were bent to their labors, widening a tunnel for reasons Tomas couldn't begin to guess. None of them paid any attention to the passage behind them.

Tomas pulled out his sword. He couldn't sneak past

them, and even if they were willing to let him pass, he had no desire to leave threats alive behind him.

Not tonight.

Whatever had made them human was long dead already.

He charged into the room, suppressing his urge to shout as he did. Two hosts fell before any even realized he was among them, victims of clean cuts through unsuspecting necks.

Though the two had died soundlessly, the others reacted to the sudden loss of their peers. They turned as one, brandishing pickaxes as weapons. Dead eyes fixed him with blank stares.

Under a starry sky, with space to move, Tomas believed he would have killed the men with ease. Unfortunately he found himself in a tunnel barely wider than his shoulders. The battlefield was tiny and dimly lit, and the hosts in front of him formed a solid wall of decaying flesh.

Regardless of their appearance, they were still hosts. They wasted away to little besides skin sagging over bone, but they moved faster and struck harder than any human could match.

Tomas let them come, hoping they would spread out a little in their attempt to kill him.

His hope was misplaced.

When they charged at him, it was all at once, like the legs of one of the spider-like sagani. Tomas cut the leader down, then danced backward as the rest of the charge reached him. The hosts swung their pickaxes without regard for life or limb, either theirs or their companions'.

The tunnel filled with bodies pressed together and sharpened steel. Unable to make clean cuts, Tomas resorted to stabbing his assailants. He aimed for vital organs, hoping he could cause damage faster than they could heal.

The man currently leading the pack took a pickaxe in the shoulder from behind. He didn't even falter as blood poured from the wound like wine from a leaking cask. Tomas angled his blade toward the man's lung. As blood burbled from the man's mouth, he swung his shovel with enough force to crack bone.

Tomas leaned back, the shovel passing before him. Then he ducked as one of the men near the back threw a dull dagger at him.

He stabbed, parried, and retreated as necessary. Losing ground didn't bother him in the least. The winner of any fight was the one who walked away.

Pride had little to do with victory.

The bloody affair took too long to finish. Hosts weren't good at knowing when they were supposed to die, and this group, in particular, embraced that quality more than most hosts Tomas had fought. But eventually they succumbed to their wounds, and it was done. The stone floor was slick with blood.

Tomas picked his way through the carnage, ensuring each host was well and truly dead.

"Hanging on?" he asked.

"Barely," Elzeth said.

There was little point in secrecy anymore. The monster knew he was here.

Tomas proceeded down the tunnels as fast as he dared, torch held aloft. The tunnels bent and turned, and then he saw a light up ahead, unlike any light he'd seen before. He ran toward the light, emerging into a tunnel that defied every reality he knew.

The stone here was smooth. Too smooth. Even the finest

artisans armed with an excess of chisels and time could match this.

Tomas found himself not in a tunnel, but in a hallway hewn from stone. Two parallel lines were embedded in the ceiling, glowing a soft white light that illuminated the hallway. Tomas glanced over at his torch and extinguished it. He stared, open-mouthed, at the ceiling.

He'd heard rumors of the achievements the church had made out east. Of light without fire.

Was this like that?

It couldn't be the same. The light he'd heard about hadn't made it west of the Tershall River. And even if it had, it wouldn't be this far west, buried underneath a mountain no one had even bothered to name.

Tomas heard Lyana, an ear-piercing scream that echoed up the tunnel.

He ran toward the sound, ignoring the mysteries he passed with every step. Images had been carved into the wall with a level of detail he didn't have time to appreciate. In one, a creature flew over the mountains.

The hallway turned, and Tomas almost fell as he took the corner too fast. There was a room at the end of this hallway, lit by the same mysterious light.

Tomas charged into the room at full speed, skidding to a stop when he came face to face with the monster.

It had been terrifying enough the first time he'd seen it. But under the bright unnatural illumination, its nightmarish aspects nearly caused him to lose the strength in his legs. Its single eye looked up at him, stripping him of pretense. Something slick glistened across its tentacles.

Four of those tentacles held Lyana in place on some sort of stone table. She fought helplessly against them. Her back arched and he saw her muscles strain, but there was nothing she could do. It was far stronger.

In the corner of the room, Colvin moved, drawing two long daggers as he stepped forward.

Lyana screamed again, and Tomas feared that he was too late.

34

Tomas darted toward Lyana, but Colvin moved just as quickly and had the better angle. The host stood between Tomas and Lyana, eyes wide with the ecstasy of revelation. Tomas drew up short to better use the extra length of his sword.

He cut at Colvin, a tentative strike to test his opponent.

Colvin had little interest in playing games. He slid away from Tomas' cut and drifted closer.

Tomas leaped backward, giving up precious space to stay alive. The daggers missed, but Colvin patiently advanced, his weight shifting subtly, preventing Tomas from predicting his next move.

Tomas held his sword out, parallel to the ground. He hated the stance, but it was the easiest way to keep Colvin away while Tomas studied his enemy's technique.

Colvin closed the distance, and when Tomas changed angles to keep Colvin away, the man somehow got even closer. Tomas blinked and retreated, pushed ever farther away from Lyana.

Impatience and frustration got the better of him. Tomas

reversed his retreat, launching an assault that should have routed an entire squad. But Colvin was never where he belonged. By all accounts, Tomas' sword should have cut him half a dozen times.

Instead, all Tomas earned for his efforts was a slightly bemused look on Colvin's face.

Tomas advanced again, and this time Colvin gave him a nasty cut on his left arm for his trouble. He didn't think he had ever fought anyone with a similar style. It wasn't that Colvin was too fast. Tomas saw his moves clearly. They just failed to follow what a lifetime of training had taught Tomas to expect.

Colvin definitely hadn't been one of the ordinary believers the church preyed upon. He'd been a knight at least, if not something even more terrifying.

Lyana didn't have the time for a protracted battle. She still struggled against the monster.

Tomas asked Elzeth for more.

The sagani hesitated, but just for a moment. Tomas retreated several more steps to make sure he would have space if Elzeth temporarily lost control.

Strength flowed into Tomas' limbs. Colvin still advanced, but his pace was slower.

Tomas attacked.

He discovered Colvin's secret. He saw the way the man's eyes caught Tomas' moves the very moment he made them. The churchman's body shifted, preparing for the strike.

It wasn't speed that made Colvin dangerous, but prediction. The knowledge gained from hundreds, if not thousands of battles, used to anticipate the future.

Tomas wasn't sure he could confuse Colvin's senses. There were only so many ways to kill a man with a sword, and he suspected Colvin had seen most of them. But there was no need. His skin felt as though it was on fire. He was faster, and Colvin wasn't prepared for his additional strength.

The difference wasn't much, but it was enough.

Tomas passed Colvin's guard and sliced him from shoulder to hip.

It wasn't an immediately fatal cut. Against a host, it might not be fatal at all.

But it took Colvin out of the fight for a few precious moments, and that was all Tomas needed.

He crossed the room toward Lyana. One of the creature's tentacles snapped at him like a whip, but he dodged to the side.

The sagani had too many limbs, though. A second tentacle caught him in the side, spinning him around and giving the first tentacle another clean look. It hit him hard, doubling him over. Blood seeped from underneath his shirt, and it felt like a bruise the size of a fist was growing just above his hip.

He lunged for Lyana, and another tentacle tried to slap his hand away. Tomas saw it coming, though, and managed to catch it.

That was a mistake.

The world around him vanished, replaced by a flood of sensations assaulting his mind too fast for him to comprehend. He stood underneath a waterfall of experiences, trying to catch a single drop of water. Images and sounds crashed over him, blinding and deafening him.

In a world where nothing made sense, he focused on one familiar sensation.

The presence of another. Invisible and unheard, but beside him all the same.

Elzeth.

Tomas extended his hand as it was buffeted by powerful forces.

Forces that wanted to tear him from Elzeth.

He groaned and stretched further, fighting for every inch. Something solid took his hand, and Elzeth was there.

Together, they fought back, seeking some way to lasso the tornado of sensation that threatened to tear them apart.

The assault never lessened, but with Elzeth's help, Tomas forced some space between him and the storm. It still raged, but now the partners watched it, as though behind a pane of thick glass.

The flood of images slowed enough for Tomas to make out individual scenes. A sagani, shaped like a leopard, making a home in the forests around the mountain. The call of something from within the mountain. It took a new form, the spider shape now so familiar to Tomas. It climbed, then descended through cracks in the mountain. It reached a light, glowing pale blue, surrounded by structures almost too smooth for the sagani to climb.

Curiosity. Then contact.

A sense of oneness, of expansive horizons both past and future. Knowledge flooded into a mind that changed and adapted from moment to moment. For the first time, the sagani *thought*, shaped by a process that wasn't supernatural, but might as well have been.

With thought came possibility, as well as fear. It imagined futures, and in some of those futures, it no longer existed.

It wanted to exist.

Survival had always mattered.

But now, it understood why.

More glimpses came, faster now, Tomas' moment of control lost. The first prospector the sagani came in contact with. The realization of what it could do. The understanding that it could sidestep death.

Tomas felt the anguish when the host began to decay and burn out, the body and mind too weak to sustain the sagani.

The wall that separated the pair from the storm shook, space warping and twisting as it endured fantastic pressures. Tomas held tight to Elzeth, and Elzeth wrapped himself tight around Tomas.

Then the storm was gone, and Tomas was standing next to Lyana. The sudden transition dazed him.

Tentacles came at him from every direction, and he flung himself away before any of them could take off his head. Pain shot up his side as he hit the floor, but he ignored it as he came back to his feet, sword in hand.

He planned on chopping the next tentacle that came his way.

But it was Colvin that came instead, lit sticks of explosive in his hand.

The sight froze Tomas in place. Never again would he allow himself to be trapped underneath the mountain. Never again would he live to survive through such a hell.

The sagani seemed to share the opinion. It picked Lyana up and rushed toward a door on the other side of the room. Lyana screamed Tomas' name, but Colvin stood between him and the rapidly departing sagani.

The creature disappeared into the hallway beyond, and a stone door began descending slowly. Colvin grinned, threw the explosives toward Tomas, and ran for the door, sliding under it just before it closed.

For the briefest moment, Tomas considered running after them. But he was sure he couldn't make it. The door would shut too soon.

He turned and fled, Elzeth pushing him faster than any human could run. As he neared the first corner he leaped, kicking off the wall and changing directions in an instant.

A heartbeat later, the fuse on the explosives finished blazing. The force of the blast was dampened by the walls between them, but a concussive wave still knocked him off his feet. Dust and debris blew past him, but the light above never faltered. He scrambled to his feet as another ear-splitting crack shattered the air.

Tomas ran as the mountain began to collapse all around him.

35

Tomas sprinted as the ceiling collapsed behind him like a giant mouth closing on a tasty morsel of food. The ground trembled under his feet, and the strange lights flickered and died behind him, casting dancing shadows against the dust-filled air.

The rumble of falling stone vibrated his stomach while the staccato cracks of a mountain breaking apart stabbed burning needles into his ears.

It was all he could do to run, to keep his feet beneath him and his wits about him. Though he didn't dare look back, he was certain the tunnels collapsed faster than he ran. His only hope was for a quick death. Far better than a slow end in the darkness.

Then the mountain settled. The floor beneath his feet no longer tried to throw him down, and an eerie silence replaced the cacophony he'd run from. His ears rang, and his head felt like it had been in a giant bell while it pealed the late hour. A few small stones trickled down from the ceiling.

Tomas stopped and turned. The tunnel behind was impassable. Years of work had been erased in a heartbeat.

Remarkably, the unexplainable light still emanated from the ceiling.

"Now do you understand why I don't like being underground?" Tomas asked.

"Your position makes more sense with every passing day." He felt Elzeth's relief, no less than his own. Their combined strength sometimes gave them a sense of invulnerability against day-to-day struggles. This mountain reminded them both they were far from invincible. Much greater powers still existed in the world.

"Perhaps," Elzeth added, "it would be reasonable to suggest that you get out of here as quickly as possible."

Tomas agreed. He ran up the hallway, looking for the tunnel that had led him in.

He found it a few minutes later.

Unfortunately, he'd left his torches back in the room where he'd found Lyana. Right now, though, the darkness frightened him a lot less than the threat of the mountain dropping on his head. Besides, he'd walked this tunnel once before. It held no new terrors for him.

With that mindset in place, making his way through the tunnels proved easy enough. Before long he was outside, breathing fresh air once again.

With the freedom, though, came a choice. "Do you think she survived?" Tomas asked.

"I don't think Colvin was suicidal," Elzeth answered. "He lit that explosive certain he would escape."

Tomas believed the same. The stone door that had slid shut between them had been thick. "Which means Lyana is still alive."

"And fighting it."

Tomas glanced back at the cave. Twice now he'd gone into the mountain, and twice he'd barely escaped with his life. A reasonable man would stop pushing his luck. "I don't want to go back in there."

"I know."

He caught a glimpse of light below him. Someone was moving around in Colvin's camp.

"For a place on the edge of the frontier," Elzeth observed, "there certainly do seem to be no shortage of people around."

Tomas descended the trail to the camp. When he reached the camp, the unknown visitor was inside the tent. "Hello?" he called.

A rifle poked through the tent, followed a moment later by a tall man. He was dressed in the sort of clothes that made him appear like a prospector. Ragged and coated with grime and dust. The man Tomas had spotted earlier, through the trees.

But he was no prospector. He held the rifle with the same confidence Tomas held his sword, and he seemed perfectly at home in this camp. There'd been two cots in the tent. Tomas had barely noticed it at first.

It made sense. Colvin was important. They wouldn't send him up alone.

"You're a knight," Tomas said.

"Knight commander, actually. Name's Ethan. And you're Tomas."

Tomas' eyes narrowed.

"Colvin told me your name when he came through with the girl. Don't think he realized who you were, though."

Tomas watched the rifle, but the tip remained at rest and pointed away from him. "Don't recall ever meeting before this week."

"We haven't. But word of your deeds has spread through the west. I'm not sure there's a knight commander west of the Tershall that hasn't heard of you."

Tomas shifted his weight, preparing for the fight he was sure was coming.

"I have no intent of dueling," Ethan said. "As much satisfaction as it would bring me, we have a more pressing problem."

"The sagani at the center of the mountain."

Ethan nodded.

"Aren't you all on the same side? Colvin just about killed me down there."

Ethan snorted bitterly. "Colvin has lost his faith. He's no ally of mine, not anymore."

"You just said you spoke as he came through. That was earlier today."

"Just because he's no friend doesn't mean I can stop him. Your reputation is well known, but here you are, your tail between your legs. Neither of us can stop him alone, as much as I'd rather just put a bullet between your eyes, then do the same to him."

"What happened? Why are you two even up here?"

Ethan gestured to a pair of stumps around a campfire ring. "Let's eat, and I'll tell you."

"We don't have time."

"I'm starving, and it will only take a few minutes. Besides, it looks like you could use it, too. You're barely standing straight."

Something in the tone of Ethan's voice caught Tomas' attention. The man didn't seem a fool, and it seemed odd to want to take a break for food. Unless— "You're a host, too."

Ethan nodded, looking less than pleased Tomas had guessed.

Tomas sat. A quick break would do him good. He would need to be at his best to fight Colvin again, not to mention the creature.

Ethan brought out food, and they both tore into it.

Ethan began his story.

"I was assigned by a bishop to accompany Colvin on a journey west. My orders were simple enough. I was to keep him safe and perform whatever services he required."

"Who was he, to earn such treatment?" Knight commanders were the best warriors the church had to offer. They didn't take orders from many, and they certainly didn't act as guards.

Ethan refused to answer that question. "To make a very long story short, our project brought us out here, to the frontier. We spoke with Tatum, while traveling incognito, about the mountain, and his claims intrigued us. We came up here. Then Colvin almost died."

Ethan paused his story to take another enormous bite of food. "Didn't see the first part, myself. Heard a scream and found him broken at the bottom of a ledge. Later, he told me he'd been pushed by a sagani, but I can't confirm that part. I saw the sagani approach, and then there was light, and he was a host."

"Why didn't you kill him?"

"His position in the church makes that problematic," Ethan said. "I hoped, that once he came to his senses, he would kill himself. Instead, he started raving about visions and the future. Then, one night, he slit my throat while I slept."

Tomas almost choked on his food.

Ethan grinned, but there was no humor there. "As I bled out, the sagani came for me."

"And you accepted it?"

Ethan sighed. "I've thought often about that moment. Part of me fears I accepted because I was afraid to die. It came too suddenly. At the time, I told myself it was because I needed to stop Colvin."

Tomas almost mocked the commander, but held his tongue. Becoming a host went against all the man's beliefs, and yet no host could be created without the unspoken consent of both parties. Ethan's faith had been tested, and he had failed. From the look on his face, it was a failure that would haunt him for what few days he had left.

Tomas focused them both on the task at hand. "What are they trying to do?"

"It wants to leave the mountain. It believes it needs Lyana to do so. I couldn't tell you why."

Tomas was skeptical. "Don't you share a connection with it?"

"I do. But if I open myself to it, it becomes too hard to resist. Even now, I hear a whisper in the back of my mind telling me to kill you."

"Wouldn't that be true, regardless?"

Ethan chuckled. "It would. It's a strange world where I need to fight against the very instincts I've spent my life developing. Where I need to ally with a man the church wants dead."

"And what if we kill it? What then?"

"Then I'll try to kill you. If I succeed, my last act will be to turn the gun on myself."

"I think you're supposed to offer to let me go free."

"Why lie? You know as well as I do you can't defeat it alone. You'd much rather take your odds fighting me after."

He wasn't wrong. They weren't allies by choice, but by necessity. "So, how do we go about this? I assume you've got a plan."

Ethan pointed up. "There's a shaft up high. It's big enough for a man to get through, but not much more. It will take you down to the heart of the mountain. Then we kill Colvin and the monster."

Tomas' stomach sank with the description of the shaft. Getting there involved a lot of climbing. And the reward was a tight squeeze back underground.

"How did you find it?" Tomas asked.

"From the inside," Ethan said. "I don't think I ever would have stumbled across it any other way."

"What about you?" Tomas asked.

"I'll follow a ways behind. I fear the monster can see through my eyes. So long as we part ways, I think you'll be able to surprise it. But I'll be there to help."

Tomas didn't trust anything Ethan said, but they did share a common purpose. It would be enough for now. "How will I find it once I'm in the mountain?"

A glitter of amusement passed over Ethan's eyes. "Don't worry. By taking this route, you'll find it without a problem. It's the only place left for it to hide. And you'll definitely know it when you see it."

They parted ways. As Tomas left the camp behind, he kept glancing back, certain he would see Ethan standing there, rifle aimed square at him. No doubt, Ethan wanted to.

For once, the creature in the heart of the mountain kept him safe. Ethan couldn't kill him before the creature was dead. But Tomas knew that as soon as he struck the killing blow, their truce would come to a very sudden end.

Ethan had described the route to the entrance well. There was only one problem. The route Ethan described went down into the forest before doubling back on itself and climbing higher. Tomas traced the path with his gaze. The only other option was to climb a nearly vertical rock face.

Neither option appealed to him.

When he saw a few creatures moving in the dark shadows of the trees, though, he knew which option he preferred. He ran to the base of the cliff and found a series of holds leading higher. He started climbing, hoping the sagani in the forest wouldn't spot him.

36

Tomas looked down at his fingers, bloody from the climb up the cliff. He breathed deeply, slowing his pounding heart from the chase. The wounds on his back and legs healed. Below him, the sagani seemed torn. At times, they would advance up the side of the mountain toward him, like a sea swelling with the incoming tide. But then they would retreat.

The monster wanted him dead.

But it didn't want other sagani to trespass on its space.

Tomas watched from a safe distance, fascinated by the ebb and flow of the creatures.

"It doesn't trust them," Elzeth said. "Whatever control it exerts, it isn't perfect."

"So why not let them close? What does it fear?"

The answer came to Elzeth a moment before Tomas realized it on his own. "The nexus."

Tomas stood up and began picking his way through the scree near the base of another slope. He stepped carefully, not wanting to twist an ankle on the loose rock.

"Do you remember when we touched one?" Elzeth asked.

Tomas bit back a glib response. Elzeth wasn't in the mood for jests. "I do."

"I wanted to become a part of the nexus. More than anything."

"I remember." The fact that Elzeth had chosen to remain hosted by Tomas had saved his life.

"The only reason I could make that decision was because of us. Because of the relationship we had built. How did *it* refuse?"

"Couldn't even begin to guess."

"Maybe it doesn't matter. One way or another, it's another nexus at the heart of our mess. Maybe it fears what happens if one of the sagani on the mountain makes the same choice."

It rang true, but without sitting across from the creature and asking it directly, there was no way of knowing. Tomas was simply grateful the sagani below didn't pursue further.

Tomas cleared the scree. He was getting close. He could hike a few hundred feet higher, and then it looked like he would have to scramble. According to Ethan, the entrance was only about two hundred feet from the summit.

Thin air made it harder to breathe, but that was the least of his problems. Soon enough he'd be descending once again.

His much more pressing concern was what happened when he reached the bottom. He had both Colvin and the creature to kill, and neither would be easy. Even if Ethan helped as promised, he wasn't sure how he'd win.

The slope became too steep for him to hike. He began scrambling, climbing up the nearly sheer face. Unlike his climb from a few minutes ago, there was little physically difficult about this ascent. Wide outcroppings and thick cracks provided plenty of options for hands and feet. Only the dizzying height proved any real difficulty.

Ten minutes of scrambling left him breathless and staring into a small, perfectly rectangular hole in the stone. His legs burned, and the slow creep of exhaustion stole the energy from his limbs. If not for the food Ethan had offered, he might not have made the ascent. He flopped down next to the hole and looked out into the distance. He was on the southeast side of the mountain, giving him a spectacular view of the range.

"You know what beating that thing will require," Elzeth said. It was a subject neither of them had broached, very much on purpose.

"Are you up for it?"

"My fear isn't whether we *can* do it. It's what happens after. If there is an after."

Elzeth searched for words of comfort, but Tomas had none to offer. He feared the same, but the only way to avoid the fate was to leave the girl behind. They'd already far surpassed the unspoken limits they set for themselves. Fighting again only hastened the inevitable.

He sighed and stood. No point worrying about it. The decision was made. "Can you kill us, if it comes to pass?" he asked.

Elzeth didn't answer for almost a minute. "I can try."

"Thank you."

Tomas felt the walls of the tunnel. They were unnaturally smooth.

Ethan hadn't lied. While wide enough to admit Tomas, it was just barely. A strong current of air came from within. Once inside, he could only move forward or backward, with just enough space to fully expand his stomach when he breathed. His heart sped up at the thought of going in there. "Together?"

"Together," Elzeth answered.

Tomas crawled into the tunnel feet first. The first segment, as Ethan had warned, was slightly uphill. Tomas crawled backwards, relying on his arms to push him back. He adjusted the sword and torch he carried so they all fit, then continued. The tunnel swallowed him.

A few feet in, the tunnel turned sharply down, and Tomas felt with his toes for the cuts Ethan promised were there. He found them, and was immediately disappointed by how tiny they were. They barely fit his toes.

Tomas let himself down slowly. The tunnel acted as something between a ladder and a grooved ramp. The angle was steep, but far from vertical.

He lost track of time and space, but it wasn't long before panic seized his heart. His grip grew sweaty and he found it difficult to breathe. Again, thoughts of getting stuck in the mountain haunted him. Recent experiences had done little to lead him to expect otherwise.

He closed his eyes and tried to imagine open spaces.

It didn't do much, but it helped a little.

He resumed his descent. His hands gripped one carved groove in the rock while his toes searched out the next one lower. Once he was certain his toes wouldn't slip, he moved his hands down. Then he'd shuffle downward and repeat the process.

Dozens of times.

If not hundreds.

The fear was always there, caged in the back of his mind, seeking any excuse to pounce.

None came. The tunnel was as well constructed as

anything Tomas had ever encountered. The fit was tight, but it never narrowed further. The grooves were always exactly spaced. He never felt at ease, but in time he gained some measure of confidence.

And then his toes were hanging over empty air.

Tomas descended farther, until his legs were hanging out. One hand at a time, he dropped down, ensuring a solid grip on each groove before moving to the next. Soon the stone pressed against his chest. He dropped one more groove and his feet touched solid ground.

Tomas let himself go, and his full weight settled on his feet for the first time in what felt like a year. He found himself in perfect darkness. He squatted down first and felt around to make sure he had space. Then he set out his torch and got to lighting it.

His hands were shaking, and lighting the torch required a few attempts.

Eventually, he had light.

He held the torch high. He was in a hallway, very similar to the one he'd been in earlier. Twenty feet in one direction, the hallway ended abruptly.

But the other way didn't end. It curved down, and Tomas followed.

The hallway was shorter than he expected. It couldn't have been more than a hundred feet before it exited onto a balcony.

A balcony deep inside a mountain. The balcony had a railing, supported by beautifully carved pillars. It was smooth to the touch, polished almost like a sword.

Tomas held his torch up and gasped.

Elzeth swore enough for both of them.

Now, he understood Ethan's cagey answer below. There was no doubt this was the monster's last refuge.

He was looking down at an abandoned underground city.

37

The sight of the city made him forget, at least for a moment, his purpose. He raised his torch high, though it made little difference. Most of the light that illuminated the impossible scene came from a glowing building near the center of the city.

At least, he assumed it was a city.

Truth was, he'd never seen anything like it in his life.

The balcony he stood on was one of several that overlooked the maze of structures. There was a cave here, in the heart of the mountain, that made every cave that had come before small and insignificant. The light from his torch had no chance of illuminating the far side.

His senses reeled from the onslaught of unreal facts. Thousands of feet separated him from the other side of the cavern, and when he glanced behind him, he saw the walls of the cavern were perfectly smooth. It was a dome.

An impossible dome.

Humans couldn't have built this. And yet the width of the hallways, the height of the ceiling, and even the design of the balcony all seemed built for humans.

A high-pitched scream came from somewhere inside the city.

Lyana was here. And she hadn't given up the fight yet.

Tomas followed a set of stairs, one eye on the city as he descended to ground level. It seemed to grow even larger the closer he came to the stone streets. Some of the buildings had to be fifty feet tall, taller than any building he'd seen before.

There was a beauty to the buildings, too, an elegance that somehow seemed even more out of place considering everything was hidden from sight.

He found no signs of life or habitation. No corpses, either. All the buildings stood tall and proud, resisting decay and instability. There'd been no violence here. He assumed that at one time, there had been a thriving community under this mountain. Then, for reasons he couldn't begin to understand, everyone had simply left.

The thought made the hairs on the back of his neck stand up.

If only these walls could speak. If only they could tell the story of what had happened here.

Tomas picked his way through the streets, alert for traps or surprises. He made his way toward the glowing light at the center of the city. It was a familiar bluish-white light, blazing like a sun under the mountain. He heard nothing.

"Do you feel that?" Elzeth asked.

The voice of his companion in his head made him jump. "What?"

"There's a breeze."

He hadn't noticed, but now that Elzeth mentioned it, he felt it as well. It wasn't much more than the slightest brush of air over his skin. That, of all things, made a shiver run up his spine. This structure was something so far beyond his understanding he didn't want to think about it.

So he didn't.

Lyana needed him.

He crossed another few buildings and came out on a main thoroughfare, twice as wide as any street he'd yet walked. It led directly to the structure in the center of the city, still glowing bright enough to illuminate most of the cavern.

Tomas walked forward. Though he supposed Lyana could be in any building, his gut told him there was only one place in this city the sagani would have taken her.

The structure surrounding the nexus looked like an arena. It was the tallest building in the city, the tops of its walls higher even than the balcony Tomas had come in on. Unlike every other building, it was circular instead of square, and several windows near the top allowed views of the entire city.

The light at the center of the area grew even brighter. Tomas squinted as a door opened and a lone figure emerged.

He'd recognize that walk anywhere. Smooth and balanced, it spoke of a deadly grace.

He put down his torch. This close to the arena, there was no need for it. Even the reflected light was nearly as bright as day. He drew his sword. The two of them stopped about twenty paces from one another.

"I'm impressed you found this place," Colvin said.

Tomas saw no sign of injury on the man's body. Only a few hours had passed. Elzeth came to life and Tomas took his stance. Colvin just smiled. "It was Ethan, wasn't it? He told you how to get here. Is he here?" He looked up at the buildings. "This would be his preferred place to fight with his rifles."

Tomas didn't enjoy the older man's confidence. "It's just me, and I'm only here for the girl."

Colvin drew his twin daggers. "She's fought, harder than anyone I've ever met. She already has a link. It was one of its offspring that made her a host. But she refuses to surrender, to give herself to something larger. Her decision brings her pain."

As if on cue, another scream echoed from inside the arena. Tomas tensed, but didn't believe for a moment he could just slip past Colvin. "Is that what you did? Surrender your beliefs?"

Colvin smiled, refusing to take offense. "If anything, my belief is stronger than ever. It's shown me the way."

"Were you an inquisitor?"

Colvin's smile vanished and he spat on the street next to him. "Nothing more than glorified torturers. Sure, there are a few clever enough to know what's important, but mostly they're just demons who take pleasure in the pain they bring others. Useful, for some of the church's needs, but they're sick all the same."

"Knight commander?"

Colvin's smile returned. "Something else entirely."

That was all the answer he gave. He came at Tomas, daggers out, swaying in that peculiar way that made him so hard to predict.

Elzeth blazed, and Colvin's motion slowed. Tomas advanced and cut, his motions as small as possible.

Colvin dodged Tomas' strike, then advanced. Tomas shifted as he spotted the attack, but Colvin was faster than Tomas expected. The older man wouldn't escape unharmed, but his wound would heal.

If Colvin's hit, Tomas would be dead.

Tomas stumbled back, off-balance as Colvin pressed his advantage. He was a bit faster than the mysterious churchman, but Colvin's experience and skill neutralized Tomas' speed.

Tomas tripped over his feet, sure he would feel cold steel through his heart in a moment.

The moment never came.

Tomas rolled over his back and came smoothly to his feet. Colvin retreated, giving him a bit of space.

"Supposed to keep you alive if I can," Colvin said. "It believes you'll join us when its work with her is done. It thinks you're something special. More so than before, now that it had a chance to share a connection with you."

Tomas growled. He was tired of the games. Tired of the mysteries. The fire inside him burned even hotter, and he knew Elzeth felt the same.

"Don't think that means I'm going to take it easy on you," he said.

Colvin smiled. "I wouldn't dream of it. But you're not the only one who has gotten stronger."

Tomas leaped at the man, murder on his mind.

38

Time.

Every heartbeat wasted against Colvin was another moment Lyana had to fight off the creature holding her hostage. Tomas stabbed, and Colvin slid out of the way, like a snake refusing to be skewered by a pitchfork. They both twisted, angling for the other.

Colvin used one of his daggers to direct Tomas' next cut away from his neck. He never met Tomas' strikes directly. He evaded and redirected, using Tomas' own strength and speed against him.

Once, a lifetime past and hundreds of miles away, Tomas had fought a student with a similar disposition at the sword school that had raised them. She'd been an older student with impeccable defense and an ability to end every fight with one decisive strike.

They'd fought five rounds.

The first four, Tomas had attacked, goaded on by youthful pride and her biting comments. He'd never touched her with his wooden sword. In return, she gave him bruises that lasted a week, much to the amusement of his classmates.

In the fifth round, he waited her out.

She mocked him, but he clenched his jaw and waited.

She stepped closer, taunting him with open targets. He relaxed his grip on the wooden sword.

The instructors threatened a beating if they didn't attack soon.

Tomas didn't care. Beatings were nearly as common as meals. The instructors always told him they had to hit him especially hard for their lessons to permeate through his thick skull.

She had cared, though. A star pupil of the school, a beating was unfathomable. She attacked him, angry at being put in such a position.

He won the fifth round decisively, returning every bruise she'd given him before the instructors ended the match.

He couldn't win this fight the same way. Somewhere, a clock ticked away the seconds that Lyana had left. Every click of the minute hand brought Tomas closer to defeat.

The temptation was to charge, to launch an attack with nothing held back. The glint in Colvin's eye let Tomas know the warrior was waiting for it.

So Tomas obliged. He'd never been much for complicated strategy.

He strode forward, a knife's edge away from unity with Elzeth. His sword flickered in the reflected light of the nexus, almost too fast for the eye to see. Colvin gave up ground, unable to remain close to Tomas' assault and stay unharmed. Tomas pressed.

Colvin slowed. The loss of speed wasn't great, but Tomas noted it. His cuts came closer before Colvin could respond.

The churchman gave up ground faster, eyes widening as he noticed the gap in speed opening between them.

The scale of the battle tipped in Tomas' favor. Little by little, he gained the upper hand, and when the final moment came, it was more of a whisper than a bang. One of Tomas' cuts was just too fast. Colvin fell too far behind. Tomas' sword sliced across Colvin's stomach.

A slow and painful death.

Tomas grimaced as Colvin fell to his knees. Colvin looked up at him. "I go to the gate satisfied with the breaths that I have taken. Will you?"

Tomas shrugged.

Colvin settled and bowed his head, presenting a clean target for the killing cut. "We always knew I wouldn't be enough. That's why we needed her."

Tomas made the cut and left Colvin's body on the street. Maybe someday an explorer would come and find it, and wonder who the lone victim of this mysterious city was.

He cleaned his sword and sheathed it. Then he ran toward the arena.

Tomas entered through the same door Colvin had left through. A short tunnel brought him to the arena's floor. He skidded to a stop.

The creature and Lyana were within, fighting the same struggle as before. But that wasn't the first detail that seized his attention. That honor was given to the arena itself. Larger than any structure he had been in, it would have swallowed the arenas out east whole. And yet its purpose was unmistakably the same. Rows of empty benches stared down at him, so vertical they almost looked as though they were stacked on top of one another.

There was a nexus here, too. It stood, tall and mysterious, at the edge of the arena floor, casting its nearly blinding light.

Tomas' fascination only lasted a moment. Then he approached the creature and Lyana, locked in their never-ending struggle. As he neared, the tentacles lashed out at him. He kept his distance, standing just outside the creature's reach.

Even with Elzeth's aid, he wasn't sure he was strong enough to defeat the monster.

"Catch one of those limbs," Elzeth suggested.

Tomas stepped back as another tentacle whipped past his face, barely visible. "I could have sworn you just suggested I touch that thing again." It had almost destroyed them the first time. He wasn't terribly interested in giving it a second chance.

It felt about the same as stepping in front of a rifle and daring the soldier to pull the trigger.

"It can't overcome us," Elzeth said. "Not if we work together." He paused. "And I'm not sure you can defeat it with your sword."

Tomas grunted. He hated it when Elzeth made good points.

He charged the creature before he could remind himself that Elzeth's idea was actually terrible. The tentacles moved too fast near the edge of their reach. Like catching a whip, his only chance was to get in closer.

The monster snapped at him, and Tomas felt his left shoulder nearly cave in under the force of the hit. He gritted his teeth against the pain and pushed on. One limb came to wrap him up, and he let it past his guard. It wrapped around his torso, impossibly strong.

As before, his awareness of the world vanished. He felt as though someone had pushed a burning poker into his mind. He didn't know where his screams ended and Elzeth's began. The assault was far stronger, far more fierce than last time.

Tomas felt Elzeth's doubt, the fear that this time they had bit off more than they could chew.

He refused to fall, no matter how hard the monstrous sagani struck.

The pressure in his head built, growing until he thought his skull might explode.

He called for Elzeth, but no one came. Somewhere in this maelstrom of sensation, Elzeth fought his own battle.

The pressure traveled down Tomas' spine to his limbs. His arms and legs felt light, the skin stretched taut over unbelievable energy.

He couldn't last much longer.

He called again, his voice tinged with desperation.

Elzeth found him. They gripped each other tightly and stood together against the assault. But even together, the strength was overwhelming. It brought Tomas to his knees.

"Don't fight it!" Elzeth shouted.

It was a terrible suggestion. The monster's strength, if not met, would tear them apart.

"Trust me," Elzeth said.

Tomas did. With his life. He let go of all his defenses. For a moment, he was sure he would die. Light filled every pore in his body.

Then the moment passed, and his mind was quiet.

He saw the monster for the first time.

Truly saw it.

It had been a typical sagani once. Until it resisted the nexus.

Now the glowing stone dominated its thoughts, had twisted its instincts beyond recognition. It reproduced, each of the spider-like sagani an eye and a limb that it used to control the area. Creatures it used to bring visiting humans to the brink of death, and then become hosts.

Tomas caught a glimpse of its dream.

It wanted to know the world.

But it didn't dare leave the nexus behind.

At first, it had believed Colvin could carry it. But the churchman's body had been too weak to contain the sagani's full power.

Thus the girl. Someone with years to burn away.

And the other hosts, to mine for the gold the creature believed it would need. The humans who hosted some small part of it were obsessed with the element. Other tunnels were built to excavate the nexus, for the stone could not be left behind.

Tomas looked upon the scenes and almost laughed.

These were not the plans of a vast intelligence. The sagani killed and maimed, but it changed its plans daily. It forgot to feed the hosts and killed them through negligence. It dreamed of ruling all humans, but had no real idea what such a goal actually entailed.

To him, it felt like the plan of a child, ignorant of the true ways of the world, filled with logical inconsistencies.

If the cost hadn't been so many human lives, Tomas could almost forgive it. If it didn't seek to control Lyana, he might have considered letting it live.

But it had to be stopped. Too many lives hung in the balance.

A single gunshot echoed in the arena.

The sagani uttered a voiceless cry that almost split Tomas in two. As his awareness of the world returned, he realized he was falling to the ground after being dropped. He landed on his feet in time to see Lyana also fall from the creature's grip. He sprinted, then slid beneath her and broke her fall.

The monster scrambled backward in a flailing mess of tentacles. Tomas stood, looking for the quickest way out of the arena.

Then he looked up to see Ethan, high in the seating of the arena. The knight commander held a rifle, and the smoking barrel was pointing right at Tomas.

39

Tomas leaped, Lyana groggy in his arms.

Ethan tracked him effortlessly. The rifle bucked, and a moment later, a giant punched Tomas in the back. The bullet hit under his left shoulder and tore out under his left armpit. The impact twisted him around, but he managed to keep his feet. He shifted directions as Ethan pulled the trigger again, this bullet passing harmlessly to his side.

Ethan didn't seem perturbed by the miss. He cycled the bolt with a smooth, practiced motion and took aim again.

So much for being an ally until the monster was dead.

"Put me down," Lyana said.

Her voice was stronger than Tomas expected. He looked down to see she was wide awake and alert. She was burning hot, too. Nearly as hot as him.

He'd lecture her later. For now, he was glad she could contribute to the fight. "Split up, and keep shifting directions. I don't think he can get both of us."

He had no time for anything more. He tossed her high into the air, stopped, and ran another direction. Hopefully her estimates of her own abilities weren't wrong. Ethan fired again, and again he missed, though Tomas felt the bullet whiz past his ear. Considering how fast he was moving and how far away Ethan was, the man knew how to handle his rifle.

Lyana landed on her feet and sprinted toward the wall of the arena, angling away from Ethan.

The man tracked Tomas instead, as Tomas had hoped he would. Better him than the girl.

Tomas slid behind the arena wall just as Ethan fired. The bullet pinged off the stone behind his head, and Tomas tucked into a tight ball. Thanks to the angle, he was mostly out of Ethan's sight.

Unfortunately, he also wasn't much of a threat.

He heard Ethan calmly sliding cartridges into the rifle's magazine. If the rifle was the model he'd seen in the camp, it was one with a magazine tube that held ten rounds, plus one in the chamber.

More than enough to kill Tomas before he could close with his sword.

For the moment, the scene was still. Like Tomas, Lyana crouched next to the arena wall, maybe twenty feet away. The monster had retreated into another exit from the arena, but Tomas suspected it was close. It wouldn't leave the nexus with enemies so near.

Blood flowed freely down the left side of his torso. Elzeth healed the wound as quickly as he could, but it would be a bit before it knitted shut.

He heard Ethan's footsteps, barely audible as he shifted position. Thanks to the circular shape of the arena, it wouldn't take him long to bring both Lyana and Tomas into sight.

Tomas broke from cover.

"Where you going, Tomas?" The voice was mocking, but no bullet split the air.

Tomas gave himself a bit of space, then turned and ran at the arena wall. He figured it was about eight feet tall, and like everything in this place, carved from stone. Tomas leaped, barely reaching the top of the wall.

That caught Ethan's full attention. The man fired as Tomas leaped up several rows of seating at once. The bullet sliced through the side of Tomas' thigh, a flaming line of pain. He pushed it aside as he angled toward Ethan.

Ethan pumped the lever, every motion smooth.

And why should he worry? They were both hosts, burning hot. Whatever difference existed in their martial skill, the rifle rendered it moot.

He twisted as he saw Ethan pull the trigger, but there was no avoiding the well-placed shot. It tore through Tomas' left arm, barely missing the bone below his shoulder.

Tomas slowed to a stop. Running would do him no good. He stood up straight, grimacing against the pain of his injuries. "Not very sporting, shooting at me while I was fighting the sagani."

The corner of Ethan's lips turned up in a smile. "I really did intend to wait until the monster was dead. Also figured that if anyone had a chance of killing it, it was you. I thought the man who destroyed an entire town, and who bested the blessed church and the Family both, would be up to the task."

Behind Ethan, Lyana crawled up the stairs, looking to get behind him. Ethan, seemingly oblivious, continued. "I overestimated you, though."

Ethan raised the barrel of his rifle, aiming carefully. "Doesn't matter in the end. It's wounded. So I'll kill you, then the girl, then it. Order's a bit different, but the result is the same."

"Are you sure you're not under its control?"

Lyana needed more time.

"It tries. And I won't be able to last much longer, but I'll kill it first."

For the first time, Tomas saw there were other rifles, set up just behind Ethan. He'd brought three. Clever. He wouldn't even have to reload. Just drop one rifle and grab the next.

If Tomas had any chance of surviving this, it lay with Lyana.

She bumped against a bench as she crawled.

It wasn't much, but Ethan's hearing was sharp enough to catch it. He glanced behind him as he pulled the trigger, the rifle still pointing straight at Tomas.

Tomas shifted to the side.

The slight turn of Ethan's head and Tomas' own movement caused just enough error for the bullet to miss.

Ethan returned his attention to Tomas.

As his finger tightened on the trigger again, Tomas leaped high into the air. Ethan adjusted, but not fast enough. The bullet took Tomas in the right leg, slicing through the meaty part of his thigh.

Ethan cycled the lever action, but wasn't fast enough to get his second shot off. Tomas cut down at him, and Ethan blocked with the barrel of his rifle.

Tomas' blade cut clean through, reducing the length of the barrel by several inches. But when he landed, his legs gave out and he crashed into Ethan.

The two warriors went down in a tangle of arms and legs. Tomas got his sword between them, but cut himself almost as badly as he did Ethan. Ethan kept twisting the rifle, trying to bring what remained of the barrel to bear. Once he got close, there was a terrifying heartbeat where Tomas stared down the infinite black of the barrel.

Tomas jerked his head to the side as the rifle went off. The bullet missed, but the sound deafened him. Ethan snapped the lever action down, and Tomas grabbed the hand, pulling at it and the lever so Ethan couldn't reload. Without a round, the rifle was little more than the world's most expensive club.

Ethan smashed his forehead into Tomas' nose, unleashing a torrent of blood. The technique worked, though. Tomas' grip slipped, and Ethan slammed the fresh round into the chamber.

Before he could aim the rifle, though, Tomas returned the favor. He drove his forehead hard into Ethan's nose, rejoicing in the satisfying crunch of cartilage as the nose collapsed. Even better, because Ethan was on his back, when he inhaled, it was blood mixed with air. He coughed and choked, and Tomas pounded his elbows over and over into Ethan's face.

He became so confident of his victory he didn't notice Ethan work his foot up along Tomas' leg until the knight commander's heel was already firmly planted against Tomas' hip. Tomas twisted, but Ethan kicked out.

It wasn't much. Tomas' twist deflected some of the kick, and all it succeeded in doing was pushing him a few feet away.

But it was enough to get the rifle in between them.

Tomas brought his sword down, hoping at the least he would kill Ethan before he died. At this distance, Ethan couldn't miss.

A gun went off.

Ethan's head exploded, blood, brain, and bone flying in all directions.

Tomas, already committed, still fell, driving his sword into a dead body.

Tomas looked up to see Lyana, rifle in hand. She calmly worked the lever, struggling a bit against the weight of the action, and chambered another round.

Tomas grunted. "Thanks."

"Figured I owed you one."

"Consider the debt paid."

Tomas rolled off of Ethan and sat up. He was covered in dirt and blood, and everything hurt.

But Elzeth burned brightly, and the wounds would heal in a few minutes. Lyana sat down next to him.

"You resisted it," he said.

"It killed my pa," she stated, as though informing him of the day's weather. "No way I was going to let it control me."

Tomas thought of the prospectors, and of Colvin. "Not everyone was so strong."

The girl had no answer to that, but he thought he saw pride on her face.

Tomas stared up at the ceiling of the enormous cavern. He still had too many questions, but for the moment, all that mattered was that he was alive, and that was good.

The thought lasted as long as it took him to notice that the monstrous sagani had emerged from the tunnel it had been hiding in. It trailed a dark brown fluid, but it still moved quickly.

Lyana brought the rifle up, but the sagani reached the nexus first. It touched the stone, which grew suddenly brighter, casting the whole world in unbearable light.

40

Tomas closed his eyes against the glare, but even with his eyes squeezed shut, his world was white.

The rifle firing next to him took a year off his life. He heard the lever action cycle, quicker than the time before. Girl learned quick.

"You even see what you're shooting at?"

"No."

"You've only got so many bullets. Use them well." As soon as he said the words, he realized they were foolish. Ethan had at least done them the kindness of bringing plenty of ammunition.

The light faded.

Tomas opened his eyes again and cursed at what he saw. Not only had the creature healed its wounds, it had grown larger. It wrapped several of its tentacles into a tight spiral, protecting the giant eye that made up such a large part of its torso. He reached out and tilted Lyana's barrel down. As convenient as it would be for Lyana to kill the creature from up here, he didn't think the rifle was strong enough.

He almost suggested leaving it alone. After his last contact with the creature, he had more pity for it than hate.

But it had killed. And he had the sneaking suspicion that if he suggested leaving it alone, Lyana would think really hard about turning that rifle on him.

He also questioned whether or not she would ever be free so long as it was alive.

Better to take care of the problem now.

Another hard lesson he'd learned far too many times.

He glanced down at his wounds. The flesh had knitted up, and although the pain hadn't faded, his limbs would work, at least for a while. He stood up, testing his weight. His legs held. He rolled his left arm in a giant circle. He grimaced as the new flesh stretched, but it would hold.

Lyana made to stand up, but he motioned her down. "Stay here." When she glared at him, he added, "That rifle is more use to you up here. If you get clean shots on that giant eye, take them. Otherwise, let me try."

She nodded. "Maybe stay alive, if it's possible."

"I'll do what I can."

He walked down the stairs, then climbed over the wall and dropped to the arena floor. The creature shifted to watch him as he approached, keeping the shield of tentacles between Lyana and its eye.

Down here, it appeared even larger. Those tentacles had been trouble before, and he guessed they were at least another foot longer than they had been. "Ready?"

He felt Elzeth brace himself. "Just give the word."

Tomas drew his sword and took one last look up at where Lyana sat, rifle braced against her knee, the barrel held as steady as the mountain they fought within. "Now," he said.

No matter how often he united with Elzeth, the experience always caught him by surprise. All the memories, emotions, and beliefs that defined him faded. The boundary that kept him and Elzeth relatively unique individuals dissolved, blending them into something more. It was thrilling and terrifying. It was death, followed by immediate rebirth.

Reason and thought faded along with Tomas' identity. He had no plan, no brilliant strategy. Life was reduced to its simplest components. Act and react.

He attacked, and his hearing was so sharp he heard Lyana's sudden gasp as she witnessed his speed. In their short time together, she'd never seen him fight like this. Few people had, and most of those were too dead to talk much about it.

The creature defended with the tentacles not being used to shield its eye. Tomas lightly hopped over one as it whipped at his ankles, then cut cleanly through another that tried to take off his head.

The sagani roared, and its remaining unharmed limbs became a chaotic storm of slimy flesh. Tomas advanced into the storm, his sword cutting at every available target. Two limbs fell, followed by a third.

Against Tomas' greater threat, it surrendered its shield. All its limbs came for Tomas, and even as he was, he was overwhelmed. He carved a chunk off one limb, but another caught him across the chest.

If not for Elzeth, the blow would have caved in his entire ribcage. As it was, the blow launched him across the arena, skidding across the stone floor like a flat rock skipped across a calm lake by a child. The back of his head cracked against the stone, and bright lights flashed in his vision.

Lyana fired, and Tomas clenched at his stomach as the

sagani roared. She'd struck true, even if it hadn't been a fatal blow.

He lifted his head in time to see the monster form its shield of flesh once again and reach for the nexus. When it touched, the world went white. Tomas used the moment to catch his breath.

As soon as the light faded, he was on his feet. The sagani had grown again. Perhaps not as much as before, but a noticeable amount. "Again!" he shouted.

He could almost feel the creature's hesitation. Now, perhaps for the first time, it fought enemies it couldn't easily defeat. It didn't want to leave the nexus, but so long as it remained in the arena, they could attack it. If it defended against the rifle, Tomas would cut it to pieces. If it fought Tomas, it left itself open to Lyana's unwavering aim.

Tomas knew, instinctively, what he would do in such a situation.

The sagani, it seemed, thought the same.

It moved with incredible speed, the eye and torso remarkably stable while the tentacles pushed and pulled it forward.

Lyana shot, missing the eye but hitting one of the tentacles.

The sagani and Tomas met in the middle of the arena. He bobbed and weaved around the tentacles, cutting them whenever he could. When two came at him at once, he switched to a one-handed grip on his sword, cutting at one while catching the other.

Unified, Tomas still felt the wave of sensation that came from contact with the creature, but it was something less, like hearing the crashing of the waves far off. It lacked the immediate ferocity of the earlier attacks.

The creature strained against him, but Tomas held firm.

The muscles in his arm, legs, and torso flexed against its incredible force.

It couldn't overpower him.

More limbs came, and Tomas ignored them, sliding closer to the giant eye. One tentacle tried to wrap around him and he jumped high. The creature tried to whip him out of the air, but he twisted and kicked the limb, using its force to redirect him closer to the center of its body.

He found himself directly before the eye, staring straight into the heart of the malevolent being.

The temptation to join the creature was stronger than ever. It promised him the peace he'd been seeking for all these years. Not the peace of isolation, but something deeper and more lasting. An inner peace, equally powerful whether he was alone or in a cloud.

There was nothing he desired more.

All he had to do was surrender, one last time.

Tomas had a tear in his eye as he drew one deep breath and made his most powerful cut, a form that drew on every bit of his power as a host. The blade cut through the eye, the force of the cut so great the eye split far deeper than the length of the sword.

Then Tomas landed amidst the tentacles and ducked to the ground as the creature wailed. Lyana fired.

And fired again.

And again.

The bullets tore into the eye of the creature, shredding the inside of the organ Tomas had so helpfully opened.

The sagani's shriek of agony and loss shook the mountain. Like many humans, it quailed before the realization its death was nigh. The shriek grew, echoing off the hard stone, until Tomas swore he'd never hear another sound ever again.

Then it ended, dying a sudden death as Lyana fired once more.

The sagani's corpse collapsed around him, finally still.

EPILOGUE

Tomas groaned as he slid out the last few feet of the narrow tunnel into the open air.

Never again.

He didn't care if an entire sisterhood of attractive women in need called for his help. If they even had one foot in a cave, he promised himself he would pass them by. He lay, flopped on the rock, staring up at the sky, beautiful puffy clouds floating so close he swore he could touch them.

The laughter started deep in his stomach and grew, spreading like an uncontrollable disease through his entire body. He laughed so hard it almost brought tears to his eyes. He felt light and free in a way that made no logical sense.

Elzeth must have felt something the same, because for once he didn't make fun of Tomas.

A muffled voice came from inside the tunnel. "Move your stupid feet!"

Tomas left them, just for a moment, solely to irritate her. Then he moved them and she slid out as smoothly as a snake. Whether or not it had been by birth or experience, the girl seemed born to live underground. She'd wanted to lead the way out, but secretly, he hadn't wanted to be left behind. He would much rather endure her constant criticism of his slow progress.

He sat up and scooted over so that they could look out over the mountains together. This one wasn't the tallest in the area, not by a long shot. But it still provided spectacular views.

It was as good a time as any to ask the questions he'd avoided earlier. "Do you still feel it?"

She shook her head. "When it went silent down there, it went silent in my head, too."

That was good. The mountain had stolen any chance she had at a normal life, but at least she had one less problem now. "What will you do next?"

She didn't answer for a good while, content to look out over the mountains above and the valleys below. Her answer was surprisingly hesitant. He'd grown used to her making decisive plans. "I'd like to travel with you, if I may."

Tomas had feared she might have something like that as an idea. He'd sworn he'd seen a look in her eye as they made their way out through the abandoned city that made him think it was on her mind.

"I don't think that's a good idea."

"You're a good man," she said, then reconsidered her statement. "At least, most of the time, I think. You keep your word, and you treat me like an adult. That's a far sight better than most anyone else I know."

"I don't have any part of my life figured out enough to care for someone else. Hells, I can barely care for myself, most days."

She chuckled at that. "No one has any part of life figured out. Those who think as much are lying to themselves."

Tomas looked over at the girl.

No.

He looked over at the young woman next to him, far wiser than her years should allow.

After all they'd been through, he found he respected her. She could hold her own in the wild, and had the courage necessary for success in any endeavor. She deserved a better future.

One that put him far in her past.

He shook his head. "I've traveled alone for a long time, and I think it's best I continue to do so for a while. I'm honored that you'd think so well of me, but it wouldn't be wise. You'll go further on a different path."

She sighed. "You won't reconsider?"

"I'm sorry, but no."

If she was disappointed, she didn't let it show on her face. She turned the question back on him. "What will *you* do?"

"Get you someplace safe. Beyond that, I'm really not sure."

"Not going to keep searching for your own place?"

He gave a sad smile and shook his head again. "Don't think that's in the cards anytime soon."

She looked like she understood.

"How do you feel?" he asked.

She turned her gaze to her hands. "Good." She met his questioning look. "Really good, actually."

She stood up and stretched. "I don't think I'll ever be able to go back to life as it used to be." She paused. "You understand that much at least, don't you?"

Tomas nodded.

He most certainly did.

. . .

FIVE WEEKS Later

AS REMARKABLE A MACHINE as the train was, Tomas decided that he hated it. It lacked soul.

Perhaps it was a romantic notion, but to him, swords had always had a heart, something beyond explanation that he completely believed.

He'd met evil swords before, as well as noble ones.

Not trains. Trains simply existed. Given half a choice, he'd choose to walk, every time. Or ride a horse, if speed mattered. But trains were also the fastest way to get from one part of the country to another. And Lyana had a lot of miles to put between her and him.

The train whistled, and the conductor made a last call for any passengers.

For the first time since Tomas had known her, Lyana looked nervous.

"You'll do fine," Tomas reassured her. "You know what you want, and that's a lot more than most can say. Just don't let that dream go."

She nodded and bowed deeply to him. "Thanks again."

He returned the bow. "You're welcome."

Then she jumped and caught him in a tight hug. It almost tipped him over, but he caught his balance. After a moment's hesitation, he returned it.

The conductor yelled, and it sounded like she was yelling at them. Lyana broke apart from Tomas with a sheepish grin. She climbed onto the train, and with an obnoxious series of ear-splitting whistles, it started to leave the station.

Lyana joined several other passengers in sticking her

head and arm out the window, waving at him as the train departed.

Tomas waved until he couldn't see her anymore, then turned and looked out west. This was the farthest east he'd been in almost as long as he cared to remember, and he didn't like it one bit. The frontier, as always, called to him.

He needed answers, too.

Ever since the mountain, something inside him had changed. Despite his fears, he didn't think he was developing tics. In fact, madness seemed as far off as ever.

He ate less, needed less sleep, and swore he could see better than ever. His energy and strength were higher than they'd ever been, and the aches and pains that normally greeted him in the morning had vanished.

Once, on the long journey here, he'd asked Lyana if she'd seen any tics from him. They'd been riding together from sunup to sundown for weeks. And she wasn't one to hide her observation from him. She said she hadn't.

Something was happening.

Elzeth didn't say much about it, but Tomas could feel that he felt the same.

They left the town, beginning the long journey west that would return them to the frontier they knew and loved. The church's lights hadn't reached here yet, but Tomas had a feeling it wouldn't be long. If he knew one thing, it was that he didn't want to be wherever those lights were.

Fortunately, he believed the simplest path to answers lay in the west.

Of all the people he'd met in his whole life, there was only one he could think of that might be able to help him. That might have answers about the sagani and hosts.

Tomas pulled out his sword to make sure it was still sharp.

It was time to visit an inquisitor.

THE ADVENTURES CONTINUE!

Top o' the morning!

I hope that wherever you are in the world, and whenever it is you're reading this, that you're doing well.

First, as an author, let me thank you for reading *Eyes of the Hidden World*. Whether this is the first book of mine you've read or my twentieth, I hope that you enjoyed it. There have never been more ways to be entertained, and it truly means the world to me that you choose to spend your time in these pages.

If you enjoyed the story, rest assured the Tomas' and Elzeth's next adventure isn't far off. Keep an eye out for the next book, releasing soon!

And if you're looking to spread the word, there's few better ways to support the story by leaving a review where you purchased the book!

Thanks again!

Ryan

Feb 19, 2021

STAY IN TOUCH

Thanks once again for reading *Eyes of the Hidden World*. I had a tremendous amount of fun writing this story, and am looking forward to writing more of Tomas and Elzeth.

If you enjoyed the story, I'd ask that you consider signing up to get emails from me. You can do so at:

www.waterstonemedia.net/newsletter

I typically email readers once or twice a month, and one of my greatest pleasures over the past five years has been getting to know the people reading my stories.

If I'm being honest, email is my favorite way of communicating with readers. Whether it's hearing from soldiers stationed overseas or grandmothers tending to their gardens, email has allowed me to make new friends all over the world.

Email subscribers also get all the goodies. From free books in all formats, to sample chapters and surprise short stories, if I'm giving something away, it's through email.

I hope you'll join us.

Ryan

ALSO BY RYAN KIRK

Nightblade's End

Standalone Novels

Blades of Shadow

The Primal Series

Primal Dawn

Primal Darkness

Primal Destiny

ABOUT THE AUTHOR

Ryan Kirk is the bestselling author of the *Nightblade* series of books. When he isn't writing, you can probably find him playing disc golf or hiking through the woods.

www.ryankirkauthor.com
www.waterstonemedia.net
contact@waterstonemedia.net

 facebook.com/waterstonemedia
 twitter.com/waterstonebooks
 instagram.com/waterstonebooks